The Sea Nymph's Curse

"You have stolen my birthright, my inheritance, Durril, son of Keeral. You will rue the day your father learned his art under this sea. You possess my inheritance, master wizard, and for that I will most assuredly have your life.

"*I will have my revenge!* Tomorrow you will be tried for high crimes against this kingdom, for endangering its well-being. Afterward you will die. But very slowly, Durril, very slowly—and with as much pain as I can inflict!"

———————————————

IN THE SEA NYMPH'S LAIR

Don't miss the first exciting book in
the After the Spell Wars series:

OGRE CASTLE

Published by
PAGEANT BOOKS

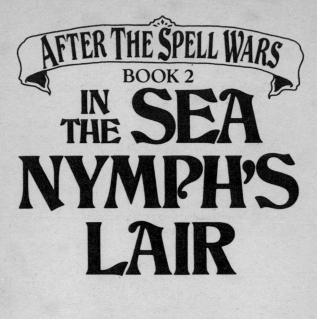

AFTER THE SPELL WARS

BOOK 2

IN THE SEA NYMPH'S LAIR

F. J. Hale

PAGEANT BOOKS

ρ

PAGEANT BOOKS
225 Park Avenue South
New York, New York 10003

Copyright © 1989 by F. J. Hale

PAGEANT and colophon are trademarks of the publisher

Cover artwork by Tim Hildebrandt

Printed in the U.S.A.

First Pageant Books printing: March, 1989

10 9 8 7 6 5 4 3 2 1

For Daddy,
who mortgaged the old Ford for the cause

IN THE SEA NYMPH'S LAIR

Chapter One

✥ ✥ ✥

DURRIL WATCHED THE calm, glassy water with a growing alarm. A sea this smooth was unusual in the Plenn Archipelagoes. It was most disturbing now during the storm season.

Since leaving Lord Northdell's preserve of Loke-Bor four days ago, the company had traveled this becalmed water under clear skies and good winds for two of those days.

"It's not right!" Durril muttered aloud to himself, his wizard's insight irritated by something just beyond his detection. "Someone ... some *thing* is behind this damnable stillness, and I mean to find out what it is."

The ocean was not Durril's realm even though his father had deeply loved it. Many times his father had tried to share the joy of it with his son. For Durril the waters surrounding the

Plenn Archipelagoes had always been a necessary inconvenience over which he traveled to ply his trade on solid ground. Now he was confronted with a puzzle that itched at him as if he were covered with brine.

Twice, very carefully, he had cast spells to reveal the cause of the unusual tranquility. For reasons he could not put into words, the wizard felt compelled to approach the conundrum cautiously to prevent his own detection.

His circumspect work had been futile. Twice he had been presented with a perplexing blank to his probings. The fair weather appeared to be natural.

But Durril remained uncomfortable. It was the season for foul weather. Even in the calmer times of the year, the Mother Ocean had never been so placid.

Morasha hugged the rail to Durril's left. Violently ill, the familiar could do little more than groan protests to anyone who came within earshot. Her giant ogre body rebelled against the movement of the ship even on this tranquil sea. The healing spell he had cast for her lasted only a few minutes.

That made Durril decidedly uneasy, too. He had once considered being a healer. He had the talent for it. Instead he had chosen the more adventurous life of itinerant wizard, exorcising the ghostly—and often ghastly—remnants of the Spell Wars. He smiled to himself. This self-imposed task was a kind of healing.

But Morasha's lingering condition affirmed his sense of foreboding. Something was not right about this too-comfortable ocean.

Arpad Zen stood morosely by, ineptly fidgeting between the ill-tempered Morasha and his frustrated master.

Durril left his companions in the stern of the vessel and paced toward the foredeck. He could find no trace of leftover remnants from the Spell Wars which had devastated the world so thoroughly. The wizard glowered at the unruffled waters encircling him and the ship, then shifted his gaze to the unclouded noon sky. He shook his head. Everything was perfect—too perfect.

Sails billowing full in the unfailing breeze, the *Pitcairn* moved swiftly toward her destination. She was laden with Durril's treasure, payment for successfully ridding Lord Northdell's castle of its murderous ghostly inhabitants. The sweating crew worked about the decks under the suspicious eye of Captain Crayken

Durril studied the officer with a jaundiced eye. He did not like the captain. He believed that crafty Lord Northdell had taken the opportunity to rid himself of one last problem by providing Durril *this* ship to carry his extorted payment.

Crayken was too quick with the cat-o'-nine tails and too fickle in his judgment for easy liking. Durril suspected that he drank on duty, too. The *Pitcairn* was not a happy ship, nor was it a tidy one, but that was the least of Durril's concerns. He turned his attention once again to the brooding calmness of the sea.

"Master," Arpad Zen whispered as he came up behind Durril. "I do not like the look of things. It's Morasha. She will not let me come near her. She blames me for her unhappy condition," Zen said in self-pity.

Distracted, Durril reviewed his arsenal of spells once more, searching for the one that would reveal what was behind the peacefulness of the waters without betraying his scrying. Something was there; he was sure of it!

"Her ogre body is the problem, Arpad. Since becoming completely physical, it has become oversensitive and does not tolerate sea travel well. Morasha will be all right when we reach Wonne," Durril answered, preoccupied with his search.

Momentarily the wizard was caught by the memorable delights of that lovely city, the trading center of the Plenn Archipelagoes. Darkly, almost in premonition, he wondered if he would ever reach port to spend his treasure on entertainments from women of unmatched beauty and amorous skill.

"Leave Morasha be for now," he instructed Arpad Zen. "Is she still aft?"

"She is lying on the deck. Durril, I really think you should have a look at her."

Something in the apprentice's voice brought Durril's full attention to Morasha's condition. They were still three days' journey from Wonne. The wizard did not want to lose his familiar. Not only had she proven useful in his exorcism, he had developed a fondness for her. In the ogre's body she was captive to seasickness and perhaps something worse. But what?

"Let's have a look," he said as he started to lead Zen toward the ship's stern.

"If it's all the same to you, Master, I'll stay here. Morasha is sick, but I think she would throttle me if I got too close to her now." Zen looked about to see if any overheard before proceeding. "And there is something else . . ."

Before Durril could ask what troubled his apprentice, a command rang from the crow's nest.

"*Now!* If ye be men! Let's serve Crayken's guts to the hungry fishes!"

The crew on the deck exploded into action. Durril and Zen found themselves fighting back to back against bollards, boat hooks, and belaying pins wielded by the *Pitcairn*'s unsavory lot.

Master and apprentice moved in harmony as they thrust and parried with the unskilled crewmen. It was easy enough to keep the sailors at bay, but the mutineers were too numerous to dispatch.

Durril deflected a cargo net thrown at them from atop the forecastle. With a blindingly fast slash of his sword, he sent the net sprawling away from them as Zen ducked out of its way. On three sides the net lay in a tangle on the deck. The uneven footing it provided prevented Durril and Arpad from going on the offensive, stranding them in the center of the angry circle of mutineers. Uneasily the attackers contained the wizard and Zen, preventing their escape but making no effort to kill them.

No sooner had the mutiny started than it was over.

"We've got the blighter, mates!" came the triumphant shout from the bridge proclaiming the crew's victory.

Captain Crayken stood in his accustomed place by the helm, but now he was trussed like a pig ready for slaughter. His eyes darted about, looking for allies. Finding none, he called to Durril.

"Wizard, you must save me and the *Pitcairn* if you wish to reach Wonne with your treasure. Use your powers. I can pay!"

Turmoil erupted once more as the burly mate knocked the captain unconscious with the hilt of his cutlass. Finished with his former commander, he motioned toward the wizard and his apprentice. The crew surged forward, weapons lowered for the kill.

Durril and Zen met the new attack with adept parries. A boat hook narrowly missed Arpad Zen's face as he stumbled away from it to collide with Durril, upsetting his master. Durril slipped to his knees before recovering. Once more Durril and his assistant were stalemated. The circle surrounding them tightened as it was reinforced by new members.

"Do not be hasty, wizard," the mate called to Durril from the bridge. "You will work for us now unless you can sail this ship by yourself. And we'll have the treasure, too! It's owed us for what Crayken has taken out of our hides with his murderous whip and his maggot-filled gruel."

"Watch your tongue," Zen shouted angrily. "It is foolish to speak to my master in such a rude manner."

"We have nothing to lose, you sniveling lackey," the mate bellowed at Zen. "We mean to give Captain Bloody-hand Crayken a taste of his own medicine before we butcher him. We can include you in our little party, too."

"Easy, Arpad," Durril cautioned his apprentice as he sheathed his sword. "Volatile situations and desperate men do not require a spark to soothe them." He pulled himself up to his full height and used his deepest commanding voice. "You there," Durril said, addressing the mate. "What is your name? I will not work for a man whose name I do not know."

"Chrestain to you, wizard," the mate answered. "*Captain* Chrestain now."

"Well, Chrestain, whatever grievances you have with Captain Crayken, you have none with me. The treasure in this ship's hold belongs to me and my confederates in payment for our arduous labors. It is not yours to take."

Chrestain laughed harshly. "I thought you might see it that way, wizard. Since you insist, I will persuade you to cooperate."

A bedraggled Morasha was hauled up onto the quarterdeck. Her massive body bounced and tumbled down the ladder, her legs crumbling like stale bread under her. She glared at her captors but could do little else. Another violent wave of convulsions wracked her immense body.

"We'll cut her smelly throat, wizard. You can watch if you like," Chrestain said, laughing. "Or will you do as I say?"

"Master," Zen whispered. "We cannot let them kill her. We have no new body for her to inhabit!"

"Do not worry, Arpad. I won't let anything happen to Morasha." He turned to the mutineer and asked gruffly, "What do you want from me, Chrestain? You have the ship and the crew. You can do what you like with Crayken."

"Mutiny is still the worst crime on the high seas, wizard. I want you to make us invisible. I want this ship and all with her to disappear until she can be refitted under a new name."

"You ask a lot, Chrestain. A cloaking spell for the ship and crew will cost you dearly. I do not believe you have the payment. I also do not believe you can get away with it. Better for you to return the ship to Captain Crayken and take your lashes," Durril replied nonchalantly. A smirk crossed his lips and he crossed his arms, sure of himself.

"Durril!" Zen shouted in alarm as Chrestain laid the sharp cutlass to Morasha's throat.

"All the payment we need is right here, wizard. If you value your friend's life, you will do as I say. And no tricks!"

Morasha's terrified eyes pleaded with Durril. She knew there was no available host body for her. The death of this ogre's body meant her final dissolution.

"Master," Arpad Zen entreated, "I will start a powerful paralyzing spell . . ."

"Quiet!" Durril commanded. "We will not use any spells if we can avoid it."

Turning abruptly from his apprentice who stared at him with incomprehension, Durril addressed the mate.

"It is not wise to threaten a wizard, Chrestain. But"—Durril interrupted the movement of the sword toward Morasha's throat"—I will do as you say. I will conjure." He made a grand, sweeping gesture before ordering, "Arpad, my bag."

The apprentice leaped through the gap in the ring surrounding them as it parted at Chrestain's nod. He returned with the kit holding the implements of Durril's wizardly trade. Durril rapidly flipped through his grimoire and found the proper incantation.

"I will need your aid, Arpad," Durril said quietly through clenched teeth. "Do as I say. Stabilize the illusion as I create it. Do not fail. Morasha's life depends on it!"

"Quit dallying!" Chrestain called as he slowly moved the cutlass from side to side in front of Morasha's throat.

"Remember, Arpad, stabilize the illusion and *don't* interrupt me!"

Durril began to work. The circle surrounding the wizard and his apprentice widened as the sailors stepped back, separating themselves from magics they did not understand.

Chanting, Durril faced the sea. Arpad Zen felt the shift and tingle of the conjuring as he followed his master's instructions. He became alarmed when he saw what the wizard was doing.

"Durril!" he cried.

"Not now, Arpad! Do as I instructed!"

"But master, I've never . . ."

"Arpad!" Durril roared, silencing his unwilling, frightened apprentice.

The master wizard finished chanting. Now he softly hummed, an odd melody which slithered about the ears and confused the mind. Zen, a strained grimace on his face, fought to stabilize the illusion his master conjured so powerfully.

The *Pitcairn* lurched, her bow lifting high out of the water. It then descended onto the surface with a loud crack as the stern rocked upward. Peace was not given to the ship. It crashed heavily back down onto the sea, jolting all on board.

A giant green and gold-scaled sea serpent coiled about the ship. It wriggled onto the deck amidship and wrapped itself around the main mast.

Pandemonium broke out as the crew panicked.

"Hold fast, men!" Chrestain shouted, gripping Morasha even tighter in the fanged face of the monster from the deep.

"Chrestain! You were saying something about killing my companion and taking my treasure?" Durril faced down the mutineer.

Zen sweated to hold the illusion which writhed about the deck and kept the crew in check. The apprentice shook from the exertion of his magical work. His grasp of the complex vision grew increasingly tenuous. Zen hoped Durril would act quickly to accomplish whatever he was going to do.

Desperate, Chrestain flung his sword at the serpent, a throw which should have struck deep into the monster's writhing coils. The sword clanged onto the deck, passing completely through the creature to lie unharmed on the weathered boards.

"A trick!" Chrestain shouted. "It's not real! Look, the sword is unharmed. It does not melt in the gorge of the damned monster. This is no true serpent!"

The apprentice could hold the spell no longer. The intricate illusion flipped from him, fading before the eyes of the mutinous crew and their captain.

Durril, who had edged toward the bridge, found himself surrounded once again, this time by men intent on his demise. Zen fought for his own life. Morasha chose that instant to vomit on the captain and the members of the crew holding her captive, scalding them with the fiery ejecta.

Free now, she tried to flee but was thrown hard onto the deck as the ship once again rocked perilously on a great wave. This time the *Pitcairn* crashed into a turbulent sea.

The roar of the water deafened everyone as the sea turned suddenly violent. Her sails ripped asunder by the instant gale, rocking out of control, her masts twisted and splintered, the ship fought the angry water.

The mainstays snapped, clearing the decks as they cracked like berserk whips in the stormy air. Groaning in a wooden death throe, the *Pitcairn* rode the tortuous waters of a mighty vortex.

"I knew it wasn't right!" Durril shouted in vindication as he stood, his green eyes flashing in the midst of chaos.

"Now, Arpad, sustain me," he called to his apprentice over the deafening hiss of the sea.

"We will need *all* our strength. The power behind this ruse is clever and almost has us! Morasha's ogre body knew all along—that's why she was so ill."

Durril fought the spell powering the vortex with all his skill. The parry and thrust of the magical match drained the master wizard's resources. But still he could not see the cunning which had created such a complete disguise. He fought blindly.

Arpad did his best to sustain Durril, but he too was rapidly failing, his reserves almost gone. The ship moaned in agony, caught between the two great forces of spell and counterspell.

Slowly Durril gripped the might behind the maelstrom. At last, with a clever, unexpected turn of spell, he succeeded in blocking the incantation, deftly removing it from his opponent's grip as if it were a sword in a fencing match.

But the *Pitcairn* could not withstand the opposing forces pulling at it.

Just as Durril wrested the rolling ship from the grasp of the enchanted sea, it broke asunder between the pounding malice of two gigantic water spouts. The vortex was replaced by the keening wrath of storm wind.

With a final loud protest as its planking ripped to splinters, the *Pitcairn* delivered all remaining hands to the unnatural turbulence of the deadly sea.

Chapter Two

✤ ✤ ✤

"HELP MORASHA," DURRIL shouted to Arpad Zen over the angry howl of the storm. "I must get to my kit!"

Durril released the spar he and his apprentice clung to. He swam hard, fighting with all his remaining strength to reach a hatch cover where his bag miraculously lay. It was precariously close to being swept into the ocean where it would be lost forever.

All the tools of his wizard's trade were in the

kit, including his grimoire and his most important treasure, the skull of his own master. Without access to the power locked in his kit, Durril stood little chance of rescuing them from the evil waters. Even if he and his companions somehow escaped the Mother Ocean, he would be severely hampered in his trade without the kit.

Weakened by combat with the power behind the vortex and the storm, the wizard gulped water, choking as he went under, only to be thrown upward then slammed onto the hatch, his head banging against a sharp corner. Senseless, he clung by instinct to the safety of the wreckage now serving him as a small raft.

Durril was unaware that the same wave which had almost drowned him had claimed his kit for the depths.

Some distance away, Arpad Zen gave up trying to direct the spar to where Morasha was floundering. Clumsily the bulky ogre fought a losing battle with the water. When Zen reached her, she was almost spent but still had enough energy to curse him.

"Stay away from me, you cur!" she groaned weakly at the apprentice. "You're trying to kill me again and leave me to the cold world of the fishes. You can't do anything right! If it weren't for you, I wouldn't be in this miserable mess."

Zen grabbed her just as she went under. He almost retched at the stench emanating from the ogre body. Water released the worst possible smells from the mottled skin.

He was barely able to hold her head above the churning, frothy sea as he tried to keep the familiar afloat.

Zen searched for something to grab but saw little debris from the ship. He had even lost Durril.

The stormy waves tossed the unhappy pair willy-nilly. Zen struggled to support the ogre, but her bulk and the unpredictability of the water made the task almost impossible. Frequently Morasha choked on the brine. He knew that if they ever got out of this watery grave, Morasha would never let him forget her discomfort—and would blame him for having caused it.

But Zen was not sure he would have to worry about Morasha's haranguing him. The water and the storm beat at him relentlessly. Too soon his hands and arms turned leaden and numb. He could barely feel the familiar in the chilly water. This time when he killed Morasha, she might have her revenge. She could undoubtedly find a haven in some sea creature or a fish. Zen could not. He would be dead.

The apprentice held on, fighting the Mother Ocean, hoping for rescue. None came as he and Morasha rode the unhappy waters late into the day.

As the last of the autumn twilight began fading, he saw that they had drifted far from the shipwreck. They bobbed alone on the vast, merciless sea.

Zen kept talking to Morasha, seeking the reassuring sound of her rancor since he could feel nothing with his hands.

"It wasn't enough to kill me three times in one day, was it?" she said chewing out the apprentice. "It wasn't enough to trap me in this gross, ugly, clumsy body when I'd had a perfectly fine dog's body or that exquisite hawk's body. Because of you, I had to endure that wretched sickness on the ship. Now you've caused me to be thrown into this disgusting water—"

"Durril will save us," Arpad cut in, having more of Morasha's reassurance than he could take for a while.

"You don't respect your master properly," she said. "Master Durril is our only chance. You certainly would bungle our rescue." They floated for endless hours. Although the storm had abated, the ocean remained rough and choppy.

A great wave broke over them, causing both to sputter and choke. Zen felt the swelling of a second wave and prepared by sucking in a lungful of air. As he looked upward, trying to time when to hold his breath, he saw the wave throw something black and substantial at them. Letting go of Morasha, he grabbed for the dark cylinder as it crashed downward.

He missed but his hand tangled in a trailing rope. As he surfaced, a bollard slammed into the side of his head, momentarily stunning him. Zen had captured a part of the mizzenmast, or more accurately, it had captured him. Both he and Morasha could ride upon it if he could find her again and pull her aboard.

"Morasha," he called frantically into the murky gloaming. "Morasha, where are you?"

"There you go again, chasing off and leaving me to be eaten by sharks." She sputtered querulously at the apprentice from somewhere on his right.

"Sharks!"

"Yes, sharks, dunderhead. They're all around us. Can't you feel them?"

A violent blow shook the mast, almost unseating Zen. The pressure of a sleek, powerful body raked against his leg. With the second blow he lost his grip and went sprawling back into the water, this time with his foot tangled in the line.

"Sharks!" Zen yelled hysterically as he clambered back onto the mizzenmast. "Morasha! Where are you?"

Again his refuge was battered, this time by two powerful bodies. The mast rolled over, dunking him. Zen had to release his grip once again to climb terrified back atop the debris.

"Don't stop talking, Morasha," he pleaded. "Keep answering me. Swim toward my voice. You must get to the mast. It's your only chance."

"Keep answering you! You are determined to drown me. You want me to keep talking so I can swallow more water, as if you haven't already caused me to swallow enough to float a navy."

"Don't preach at me, Morasha. Just swim! Come toward my voice. This is our only chance of surviving," Zen shouted urgently as the mast was struck again, causing it to shudder and buck beneath the apprentice.

"We wouldn't be in this fix if it hadn't been for you," the familiar snapped. But the sound of her voice grew louder. She swam toward him as he had directed.

"Whatever you say, Morasha. Keep swimming. I think I can see you," the apprentice said.

Then she was close beside him, ineptly splashing about but at last coming abreast of the mast.

"Grab hold," he ordered. "You can quit wasting your breath on me now. We're lucky to have this piece of wreckage to cling to. I couldn't have held you much longer . . . and with these sharks about this is our only chance." He slipped off, sputtered, then struggled in the water, legs kicking to keep his head above the churning waves. He awkwardly scrambled back onto the wooden spar. "You're lucky I grabbed it," Zen said, taking the offensive in the perpetual sparring match with the familiar.

"Of course you couldn't continue to hold me! What else can I expect from you," Morasha snarled. "As for the sharks, Arpad Zen, I've saved you from them. They don't appreciate odor of wet ogre any more than you do."

In spite of her sarcasm, Morasha held on to the mast with renewed hope as the sea and the remnants of the storm moved them toward their fate in the dark night.

"What is that?" Morasha demanded as she rudely shook Arpad Zen awake.

"What?" he asked groggily.

"That, behind you. It looks like a light in the distance. If you hadn't been sleeping—but that is typical of you at a time like this," she concluded in disgust.

Zen stared into the night at the tiny pinpoint of light. It did not move and it did not fade.

The storm had passed hours earlier. The two companions rode the mast as it bucked in the hard sea under a cloudy, moonless sky. Zen studied the light for some time. It grew infinitesimally larger and brighter.

"Morasha, that's a lighthouse. We're near land!" he cried jubilantly.

"Are you sure?" the familiar asked, forgetting to berate Zen in her hope of gaining landfall.

"It must be! The light is stable. We are moving toward it. There has to be land!" He spat out a mouthful of foul water and tried to squeeze out the annoying dampness in his eyebrows. He failed. "All we can do is ride this mast and hope the current brings us to the shore soon," he said.

"Can't you think of anything else?" Morasha asked caustically, back to her old self again. She fell silent and watched the beacon grow in size and brightness like her hope.

At last the two bedraggled pieces of flotsam heard the roar of the waves pounding on the darkness-cloaked shore. The light was to their right down the coast. They finally made out the beach as the ocean carried them swiftly toward it.

The boom of the pounding water increased as they approached the shoreline. Too late, Zen realized that it was far too loud to be the sound of waves hitting the beach.

"There is a reef, Morasha! Hold tight!" he shouted over the din of the breaking waves.

Before the familiar could retort, they smashed into the unforgiving barrier, almost losing their grip on the mast. Dragged back out to sea, they were flung a second time at the offending rock.

This time the mizzenmast broke apart against the stony undersea barricade.

"Swim for it, Morasha," Zen called to the familiar as she lost her hold. "Swim for it," he shouted again in despair as the ocean current carried him away from the reef and out to sea once more.

"If I live through this," he said aloud to himself, "she will never let me hear the end of it."

Morasha lunged up out of the water, sputtering and spitting angrily. Her shoulder was torn where she had battered it against the reef. Thick black slime oozed into the salty water from the wound. But she was inside the barrier and the sea was calmer there. She got her bearings with the light to her right and struck out for the shore.

Her ogre body had not been made for swimming. Even the buoyancy of the water did not help counter its unwieldiness. Morasha persevered, fighting the tide and the scattered rocks in the lagoon. Several times she was thrown into them, tearing and bruising her flesh each time. The body she inhabited was in growing difficulty.

At last she achieved the beach, tossed upon it like a deformed piece of driftwood. Morasha lay there for a long time, exhausted. Silently she cursed Arpad Zen.

"The fool!" she thought. "He always muddles the simplest task. Even getting us to land was too big a chore for him."

Eventually the familiar pushed herself into a sitting position and she angrily spat sand from her mouth.

"It serves him right," she muttered out loud. "He is completely inept. The sharks will probably choke on him."

When dawn pricked the eastern sky, Morasha cast about for a place to hide. She did not know whether this island was inhabited. It probably was, like most of the islands in the Plenn Archipelagoes. That would mean a hostile welcome for her if anyone saw her. Since the Spell Wars, ogres were not given gracious hospitality.

Morasha found walking difficult at first, then impossible. The seasickness and the soaking in the ocean had taken its toll on her, leaving her weak and dizzy. She crawled into a small sea cave hidden by wave-smoothed boulders. There she slept fitfully, muttering angrily only once in her dreaming.

"That fool apprentice never could do anything right!"

"What's this?" questioned a raspy voice as callused hands jerked Arpad Zen upright.

"Looks like the sea didn't throw us any treasure this time," came a high-pitched response close by Zen's left ear.

"I must be on land," he thought, the wonder of it filling him with joy. The last he remembered was clinging to the broken mast as waves battered it against jagged rocks under the lighthouse.

He had swallowed water and vomited. And he had held to the mizzenmast with all his might even as his hands were beaten between it and the sharp rocks. After that, he remembered . . . nothing.

The raspy voice sounded again, this time directly in front of him.

"Who are you? And what brings your scrawny carcass to our shore?" it demanded.

Zen opened his swollen, sand-caked eyes to see the brown, weathered face of a scraggy little man looking back at him from mercilessly cold blue eyes.

"I am Arpad Zen," he said through cracked lips, "apprentice to the master wizard, Durril."

"A wizard's apprentice, eh? Maybe the Mother Ocean has brought us some treasure after all, boys. You couldn't tell by looking at him, though."

A chorus of laughter greeted the diminutive man's remark. Zen looked about to find himself surrounded by a gang of rough, unsavory men. The mutinous crew of the *Pitcairn* were courtly gentlemen compared to this lot.

"Thank you for rescuing me," Zen said in his best aristocratic manner. Always take the offensive, Durril had battered into him during their time together. Zen decided to appeal to the venal nature of the gang surrounding him.

"I am sure my master will have a reward for each of you when he returns for me."

The troop broke out in renewed laughter.

"And when might that be?" the raspy-voiced man taunted. "After he has been served to the octopussys for their dinner?"

Zen was still being restrained by the hard grip. The hold on his upper arms was beginning to hurt. It chafed his sunburned, salt-stained skin.

"Remove your hands," Zen ordered. "I do not wish to harm you."

These statements provoked a new round of hilarity. The apprentice tried to break the strong grip that held him, but his futile efforts only brought more laughter at his expense.

He then attempted a personal defense spell but could not remember the sequence. His head throbbed and his vision turned momentarily blurry. From what he could tell, it was almost evening. He must have lain on the beach unconscious for most of the day. Nausea tugged at him. Zen gave up his effort at the spell. The headache lessened but continued to pound behind his eyes.

"I am Mister Tukker," the raspy-voiced little man said by way of introduction. "Me and my good associates here have a great respect for the sea, ain't we, men?"

Tukker's gang nodded in agreement.

"You might say that we appreciate the paltry gifts she sends us. It's a way o' makin' our fortune, you see."

"You're wreckers," Zen blurted out.

"Salvors, Arpad Zen, salvors. We salvage what the sea gives us and we sell it to make our living. We work in harmony with the more fickle elements of the Mother Ocean." He smiled crookedly and stared at Zen to see if he believed this lie. "It's an honest line of work," Tukker concluded in mock offense when he saw Zen's skepticism.

"What are you going to do with me?" asked Zen.

"You might just be our best salvage job yet.

Now look, your mate is gone. Few men survive a storm at sea, especially like the one what hit the coast yesterday. The Mother Ocean saved you and gave you to us, it seems to me." He smiled, showing broken, yellowed teeth. "What shall we do with you?" Tukker asked as he winked and nodded at his scruffy comrades.

A large, burly man growled at Tukker. "He ain't no good to us, Tuk. But he knows where we're workin'. We'll just have to kill him and give him to the crabs to nibble on. We can't take no chance that he would divulge our location."

"Yeah, Tuk," a second cohort chimed in. "This shore's been good to us. We can't let this piece of drowned rat ruin our operation. Let's kill him and get it over with."

Zen trembled. He had been saved from the depths only to be murdered by a gang of wreckers. He shook his head in disbelief, attempting a paralyzing spell. The headache banged into full force. He could not complete the spell.

"Wait," Zen croaked, his voice breaking from his parched throat. "You don't want to kill me. I am a wizard's apprentice. That's not like being a wizard—not exactly—but I do know some things."

"I dunno, Tuk." A tall, weaselly fellow spoke up. "He might be of some use. Some wizard's tricks might come in handy."

"I can do any number of tricks," Zen blathered, "and I have even employed some minor banishing spells by myself. Are you afflicted with poltergeists?"

"Quiet!" Tukker roared. Arpad Zen bit his tongue. The gang stepped respectfully back as the wiry little man paced up and down in front of the apprentice.

After what seemed to Zen an interminable length of time, Tukker stopped in front of him, jutted out his stubbled, scarred chin, and nodded slowly.

"He might come in handy. If he don't, we can always kill him later," he said in his raspy voice.

Zen was lifted bodily up off the beach and carried to the thieves' den, where he was set to cooking under heavy guard.

He was allowed to eat whatever leftovers there were. After he finished gobbling them, Zen sought to make the best of the situation. For the time being he was alive. He just had to stay that way.

Hoping to ingratiate himself with his captors, he attempted some conjurings of simple, humorous illusions. But again, his head ached and his vision blurred. Instead, he performed the sleight-of-hand tricks he had learned for the warm-up to Durril's raree show.

First he pulled stones from behind a pudgy man's ear. Then he played hide-the-button with three of the crew's cups. They liked the game and spent some time betting against one another until tempers flared and Tukker called an end to it.

For a finale, he tied knots in a borrowed scarf and challenged the owner or anyone in the group to untie them. None of the lot could get them to budge. Zen released the knots with a touch. All through the performance he was careful not to make Tukker or his top assistants the brunt of any joke.

The company relaxed into a merry evening. They even offered Zen some watery, bitter grog. Purposely he pushed away thoughts of Morasha. Too many times already he had caused her death. This time he willed her to be alive.

The tall, weaselly man refilled his cup. Perhaps life with the wreckers was not too terrible after all. It was at least drier than foundering at sea.

"Say, do you know the one about the traveling salesman and the peg-legged whore from Pin?" Zen began.

"Tie him up and gag him," Tukker ordered.

Chapter Three
✦ ✦ ✦

THIS TIME THE vortex spun smaller but not slower. No lulling pretense of fair weather surrounded it. The rapid hiss of fast-moving water and the irritating tingle of magical energy alerted Durril to its presence. No effort had been made to mask the ability behind the maelstrom.

Durril clung to the hatch cover, riding the swiftly turning spiral downward. Unable to exert any control over the swirling waters, he worked to counter the mind behind them. He quickly discovered he was too weak to break the formidable magic pulling at him. The wizard could do little but wrap himself in a personal defense spell and ride the hatch to its destination.

He reached the ocean floor swiftly. Before he could act, the Mother Ocean closed over, encasing him in inky darkness.

Surprised, Durril found that he could breathe normally. Whoever had captured him had seen to that. The power directing all this did not want to kill him . . . yet.

He tried to reach out and explore his strange, dark prison. Durril cried in panic when two giant phosphorescent squid seized him. Encasing Durril in a cage made of their tentacles, they carried him off through the murky depths.

Durril's initial fear faded and reason returned. The squid were physical. Durril confirmed this with a simple observation spell. But other, more outlandish creatures he passed in his soggy journey definitely were not.

The watery world was populated with dangerous remnants from the Spell Wars. Most of the nearby phantoms were harmless blue and green ectoplasmic pests. There were others, however, not so harmless. He was surprised when they paid him little heed.

A phalanx of mermen riding violet ectoplasmic sea horses surrounded Durril and the squid. Durril tried to greet their leader but a flash of a trident laid open his cheek. The wizard fell silent. The company made its way through the darkness with great speed. Schools of silver fish scattered before their onslaught. Although the mermen were physical manifestations, they had reached an easy accommodation with the phantom sea horses who left a fiery trail to mark the path of their travel. The

sea horses, Durril observed, were created beings, remnants of the wars he had never before
encountered.

"Even here," Durril said softly, hating those
who had gone before him. "Damn those old wizards for what they did!"

The mermen turned and dived and rushed
through the murky waters at an increasingly
dizzying pace. Disoriented, Durril could not tell
how long they traveled. As the water became
shallower, the sea-green light gave eerie shape
to the world surrounding him.

Durril found himself in an enormous cathe-
dral supported by serpentine coral pillars. The
colonnade formed an underwater grotto open
to the surface of the water. Looking up, he
thought he could reach out and touch the sky.
Living creatures, the corals pulsated with hues
from the palest rose to the deepest, most vi-
brant blue. Throughout the underwater cathe-
dral swam brilliantly colored fish, decorative,
moving accents in the exotic landscape.

The floor of the gigantic grotto sparkled
brightly with gold and gems, death treasure
from innumerable cargoes lost to this deep, wet
world.

It took a moment for Durril to get his bearings. He was taken aback by the immensity of
the hoard. Flitting through it were fish of all
shapes and design, rays of gigantic propor-
tions—and the aquatic ghosts of long-dead
drowned sailors transmuted by the ocean's
magic into pearlescent shadows. Far above
their heads floated a navy of iris-colored men-
of-war.

Durril's attention focused again on the pre-

cious debris scattered about him. Spread on the
ocean floor as far as he could see were gold and
silver coins, jewelry, sterling plate, and gems of
untold variety. Assigned to the treasure which
had been theirs during life, the pearlescent
ghosts were stationed throughout the hoard as
guards. The abundance staggered Durril's
imagination. His palms itched in appreciation
of the wealth.

Durril's two escorts deposited him before a
throne in the center of the treasure field. The
seat was made from the skeleton of some ancient bark now encrusted with luminescent
barnacles. On the throne sat a young woman,
her ankle-length red hair dancing like graceful
seaweed about her lush, pale body.

She was scantily clad in an ornately patterned
gown of polychrome scales. Durril noted that
the gown revealed a voluptuous figure. The san-
dals adorning her feet were made from small,
delicate clam shells. She vibrated before him in
the moving water, emanating a sorceress'
power—and something more.

Surrounded by bright pink ectoplasmic eels,
the sea nymph gazed on Durril with wrathful
amber eyes.

"So, you are the meddler who dares oppose
me. Step forward. I want to see you better," she
said. Her voice sounded of music, a siren's song
of ancient days luring seafaring men to their
deaths.

Durril did as instructed, finding normal
movement slightly out of his control in the watery world. He overcompensated, almost falling, but righted himself before he reached the
foot of the throne.

As he started to speak, the sea nymph stopped him with an angry wave of her hand.

"Hold your tongue. I am Rusalka, ruler of these deeps. You have caused me much trouble today. My new treasure is scattered throughout the ocean," she said angrily.

"It will take some time and effort for my minions to collect it. For this inconvenience you will be punished. You will gravely regret having fought me. Never before has anyone possessed the ability to discover and defy me. I would know your name."

"I am the master wizard Durril. The treasure you stole today is mine," he admonished, taking the offensive. "You have kidnapped me and caused the death of many good men. You are a thief and a murderess," he concluded, testing her temper with measured words.

Rusalka laughed, a sound like tinkling crystal bells. She did not immediately reply to his taunt. The sea nymph sat pensively staring at Durril. When she spoke again, her words quivered with barely contained curiosity.

"Why do I feel that I've met you before now, meddler? It cannot be so."

Durril did not know how long sea nymphs lived. Rusakla could possibly have known his father, but he doubted it. She looked nearer his own age. But maybe looks were deceiving. Who knew the affairs of a sea nymph well enough to learn?

"I have only this day been kidnapped by you, sorceress," he replied. "Had I met you before, neither one of us would have forgotten it," Durril said, his green eyes twinkling with a meaning beyond his words.

"Silence!" Rusalka commanded. Unsettled, the sorceress found her wrath mixed with an involuntary attraction to the handsome man standing before her. He filled his jerkin and breeches well.

Quickly Rusalka changed tactics. "How came you to be a wizard?" she asked.

"I am the son of Keeral, himself a master, one who learned his art in the Mother Ocean," Durril said, still watching the sea nymph for betraying emotion. He hadn't been killed outright for insolence. Durril thought he was on safe ground with Rusalka—for the moment. "I come by my trade and talent naturally."

Durril stopped speaking, startled at what he had just revealed of his lineage. He bit his tongue and tasted blood—and more. "A truth spell!" he cried. "And cunningly laid on."

He worried at the ease with which she had breached his defenses. He found her power *very* interesting . . . and very discomforting.

The sea nymph smiled at him, amber eyes ablaze with emotion he could not decipher.

"And you, Rusalka? How came you to be a sorceress of such subtlety and power?" he asked.

Not answering, the sea nymph glared him. He could feel the palpable hatred radiating from her. Durril moved his fingers, working a paralyzing spell. Instantly Rusalka raised her hand. Durril froze, unable to move.

The eels nearest to him began a loud thrumming. Stinging vibrations beat on his body. At the same time, water flooded into his mouth and nostrils, strangling him. He was unable to fight back. With a flick of her wrist, Rusalka released him to choke and gasp for breath as he expelled the water.

"Do not try that again, Durril! Under the sea *I* rule. I mean to have you punished. Do not make me kill you outright," Rusalka threatened. She gestured at him in dismissal.

The two giant phosphorescent squid returned. Again they caged Durril with their tentacles, escorting him this time to a prison cell. The pink eels accompanied them, taking up guard duty outside the small cavern that was now the wizard's lodging. Durril was grateful they had ceased their thrumming.

He let out a long sigh that caused tiny bubbles to rise from his lips. The captive wizard took advantage of his unhappy situation to rest and think. Who was the sea nymph and how had she come by such immense power without him learning of her years ago? To that he had no answer.

He waited long enough for his guards to become bored with the routine of their duty, then launched a strong soporific spell against them. The power grew and caused ripples to radiate outward from his prison cavern. The master wizard smirked. He would soon have them snoring peacefully. But as he continued to conjure, a lethargy crept into his body, squeezing out strength and forcing his eyelids to close with leaden insistence.

Durril slept long hours without dreaming as his guards swam undisturbed outside his prison.

When he finally awoke, the full puzzle of his condition weighed on him. Three times his spells had backfired. His personal defense spell

had been nullified by Rusalka. When he tried
the paralyzing spell in her throne room, it had
been turned against him. Even his soporific
spell had bounced back on him rather than ren-
dering his guards senseless, as intended.

Anxiously, Durril reviewed his spells and
conjuring procedures. The observation spell
had worked on the squid. He tried a simple
scrying spell. The image he got was muddled,
warped in some odd way so that he couldn't
read it. The same held true for his transmutation spell. He employed it on a small piece of
shell. Only lead resulted, not gold.

In disgust, Durril began pacing. As he walked,
he examined his cell. A harmless blue-green
scavenger snail clung to the wall of the cave.
Durril worked an exorcism on it. The scavenger
blinked out of sight only to reappear moments
later, still placidly clinging to the wall.

Methodically, Durril started again. He went
through his basic spells and chants to be sure
he remembered them. They were matters of old
habit, thoroughly ingrained in him by his own
master. He tested his memory of them by re-
tracing the steps his master had taken to teach
him. Durril's chants were correct, his magical
gestures, also.

What was wrong? Was it the effect of the water world on his magics? Or was it the power
of the sorceress, Rusalka, that bent the spells,
preventing them from working?

Durril resorted to the only spell that had
worked for him. He cast an observation spell
on the scavenger snail. He saw a blue-green ectoplasmic remnant of the Spell Wars and nothing more. The wizard then followed with an

exorcism spell. The scavenger dissolved into nothingness, completely gone.

Working in a fever, Durril chanted, focusing the observation spell on the eels guarding the door. They were revealed to be pink ectoplasm, also remnants of the wars. He then tried a very mild soporific spell. This time his guards were noticeably slowed.

"That is a small comfort at least," Durril muttered to himself.

"Everything seems to be tied to the observation spell. I always tell Arpad to be sure before he acts. I must take my own advice."

After Durril was taken away to his cavern cell, Rusalka sat glowering on her throne.

"At last," she said quietly to herself as she unconsciously pounded the ornate arm of the chair.

"At last I have you," she whispered to the absent Durril. "You have stolen more from me than a thousand ships laden with gold, wizard." Her face hardened. "You look like him," she said aloud. "I was very young, but I will never forget his features. The resemblance is unmistakable." Her anger grew as she remembered— much of it hurt her deeply.

"You have stolen my birthright, my inheritance, Durril, son of Keeral. Today you dared to oppose me in taking the treasure from your ship. But that is nothing. You will rue the day your father learned his art under this sea. You possess my inheritance, master wizard, and for that I will most assuredly have your life."

The sea nymph was lost in memory, a child again, scattering starfish and anemones at her sister's wedding to the human who loved the Mother Ocean. All the old jealousies, the old resentments came flooding back.

"O Vila," Rusalka begged again, "I pleaded with you not to marry him. But he enchanted you and took what was rightfully mine. You died defending him because you loved him." She held down the oceanic emotions building inside her.

"A sea nymph has no place for love," Rusalka scolded her long-dead sister.

"Because you gave your knowledge to Keeral, darling sister Vila, I have been bereft of the power which is rightfully mine! He abandoned this realm after you died, taking with him the knowledge that should have belonged to me."

Rusalka stood, all her anger and resentment focusing on the captive Durril. Her small pale hands made triumphant fists.

"You will pay, master wizard Durril," she promised. "The power you hold belongs to me, stolen from me by your father." She smiled wickedly, then laughed harshly.

"*I will have my revenge!* Tomorrow you will be tried for high crimes against this kingdom, for endangering its well-being. Afterward you will die. But very slowly, Durril, very slowly—and with as much pain as I can inflict!"

Chapter Four

✣ ✣ ✣

"Beware . . . beware . . . beware . . ."

The horrid, deafening wail rang about the assembled men, sending icy prickles up every spine.

Trevoor, Tukker's weaselly sidekick, closed the trapdoor to the beacon room, dampening the sound. The cry hurt the ears but mostly it jarred the soul.

"There may be a use for you, after all," Tukker said and smiled, showing the gaps in his broken, yellowed teeth. The heart-wrenching moaning acted as counterpoint to the wrecker's words.

"Takin' this lighthouse was easy enough, but we have a problem. You see, friend, that ain't no ordinary beacon up there. It's time you paid for your supper, lad."

Arpad Zen shuddered at the thought of the burning ghost which served as warning for the treacherous coast below. The misery endured by the specter appalled him.

Cursed at the time of his death, the man had been damned to the eternal ordeal of fire, a conflagration which never consumed him. Unless released, his spirit would burn forever. The apprentice had heard of damned specters but had never seen one. Zen quaked at such vicious punishment, his mind refusing to speculate on its cause—or if it had been warranted.

"We want him done away with." Tukker interrupted the apprentice's musings. "What you call exorcised."

"I'm only an apprentice," Zen said uneasily. "I have never done a major exorcism."

"But you've seen one, ain't you?" Tukker threatened him silently by stroking along the edge of a sharp knife edge using a dirty, callused thumb.

"Yes, many times, but . . . but that is different from doing one," Zen stammered. "I am not sure I can do it. I have no equipment. All I had was lost in the storm." Zen saw this had no effect and took a new tack.

"The exorcism . . . it can be done by the light of a full moon. That'll be in another two weeks."

"It's night and we ain't got time to fool with you no more. There are merchanters due through these waters soon. This cursed light is affectin' our business. Now put it out right now or we give you to the sea creatures for a late supper," Tukker said impatiently.

Trevoor grabbed Zen, forcing him through the hatchway into the room above where the accursed ghost was imprisoned. The wrecker bolted the hatch closed.

"Beware . . ." The miserable spirit keened, turning slowly like a top in the center of the room.

Zen fought down a fear that threatened to devour him. He covered his ears with his hands, attempting to mute the horrible call. The specter did not acknowledge him as it spun slowly, voicing its eternal misery.

"If I can manage the exorcism," the apprentice reassured himself, "it will be a boon to that pitiful soul."

Zen circled the spinning ghost. The man had been young, about the apprentice's age. He appeared full-bodied in the never-ceasing curtain of bright orange flames. The fire tortured his soul but refused to render the body to ashes.

"What did you do?" Zen whispered, more to himself than to the ghost.

"I loved where it was forbidden," the specter replied without ceasing its rotation.

"What?" Zen asked, startled by the ghost answering what he'd considered a rhetorical question.

"I loved where it was forbidden. As my liege lord's man, as his friend, I was bound in honor to respect his wife above all women. But Pellas was old and Nameha young, a marriage of incompatible seasons. He sought an heir and had not the capacity to sire one. Nameha, in despair because she could not please her lord, sought reassurance from me who was her age and Pellas' friend." The ghost flared and almost blinded Zen with the sudden light.

"We did not intend it," the burning ghost cried. "I counseled patience to her, and for her part, she strove in all ways to please Pellas. But the months passed into years and still she was without child."

"But you acted honorably," Zen said.

"Yes, honorably, until that dreadful spring. She asked to talk with me, but away from the palace. Nameha came to me on this headland which in that delightful season betrays its more sinister nature for a cloak of sweet clover and a blanket of flowers. It was late afternoon. She was distraught and sorely afraid. Pellas had railed at her for not bearing a child. He had

threatened her life because she had not produced a life to carry his name. Ah ..." The
tortured soul moaned in agony at the remembrance.

"I knew better. Still I reached out and
touched her, took her in my arms. At first, my
intent was only to comfort her, to console her
in the face of her husband's unreasonable
wrath. What had smoldered between us all
those years at last burst into flame. Even if we
had so desired it, we could not have escaped the
hot storm which ignited between us and en-
gulfed our hearts.

"We lay together on the sweet ground as one
being. When we had exhausted our energies,
unwittingly we slept. The king's guard was sent
in search of Nameha when her long absence
from the palace was discovered. In the night
they found us where we lay spent, entwined in
each other's arms.

"Pellas' nature was never one which encompassed understanding of frailty, nor did it embrace forgiveness. Rather, it matched the severe
landscape of this, his kingdom. His judgment
could not be revoked.

"Nameha was imprisoned in the tower until
her death. She was to see no person, not even
her jailers. Her food and other needs were
passed to her through a partition in the door of
her cell. When she died, the doorway was
sealed. Such was her punishment for seeking
companionship outside that of her husband's.

"In time she did bear a child—my child."

Again the burning specter fell silent, overcome by his own history. Zen stood horrified
and pale before it.

"Only once was her solitude invaded," the damned ghost said, taking up the tale again.

"Pellas came to her tower. Enfeebled with age, he was still strong enough to snatch the child from her and wring its neck. It was thrown on the dung heap."

The tortured specter gasped, choking on its story. It spat a fiery gob that burned into the night and continued.

"My punishment was different. I had been Pellas' most trusted liegeman—had been son where there was no son. And truly I had loved him, for in spite of what I tell you, he contained much that was honorable. I had also loved where pride could not ignore.

"Pellas ordered this lighthouse built on the very headland where Nameha and I had lain. When it was completed, he brought me from the dungeon to be executed. He cursed me, condemning me to burn forever in this fire which will not consume me.

"As I had burned for Nameha in life, so would I burn for her in death. I would be a beacon of her shame which would light her night and allow her no forgetfulness. From her tower, she could clearly see this light.

"As his once most trusted vassal, I was to continue serving him as guardian of this coast. I would shine as a warning to any who would breach the king's treacherous shores unaware. In this only did he allow me a kind of redemption.

"Pellas hired a clever wizard who at my execution laid on the king's curse. All that was many, many years ago. Until this day, no one has asked this tale of me. Is not my eternal torture enough that I must also recount my unending sorrow?

"Beware ... beware ... beware ..." The burning ghost gave up its story to once again issue Pellas' ancient warning.

The light emanating from the damned being cut into Zen's eyes like a thousand knives. His head ached from the assault of the blazing ghost's pain. He was shaken by the specter's tale. He vowed not to speak to it again.

Working as quickly as he could, the apprentice set about to exorcise the pitiful being.

He first tried his spell against poltergeists. It was the only one in his collection he felt confident of controlling. For long seconds after conjuring, he waited. His feeble spell had no visible effect on the ghost.

"There must be something I can do," Zen said. Not only did he sympathize with the damned man, he also knew that Tukker would return soon. The wreckers were busy setting the decoy lights, but the little man was nothing if not thorough. He would personally check to see how the apprentice's work progressed.

Tukker, Zen knew, was tiring of the raree show tricks. There was not much for the apprentice to do with the gang. He was confident Tukker looked on him more as a liability than an asset now.

Ineptly, Zen began the spell Durril had used on the magician ghost in Lord Northdell's castle. Twice he forgot the sequence of the chant and the hand movements and altered them to the point of failure.

He started a third time, making swift work of the spell, but stopped short of finishing it.

"I don't know the end," Zen said, irritated at himself. "Why didn't I pay more attention!" he chided himself, hearing the echo of his master's voice.

At a total loss, he fidgeted about the deck of the beacon room. As he paced in the confined space, he inadvertently stepped into a water bucket. He fell and banged his head against the railing encircling the room. Even more humiliating, his foot was stuck firmly in the bucket. Sitting down and struggling, he finally freed it. In the meantime, he had set up quite a clatter in the lighthouse tower and soaked himself in the process. The night was chilly and wind gusted through the lighthouse, causing Zen's teeth to chatter. If he had ever been more miserable, he failed to remember the time.

"Of course I would have to get wet," he moaned, "and nothing to show for it!" He paused, his mind spinning through myriad possibilities for spells.

"Why would there be water buckets in this tower?" he mused. "The ghost can't be doused by water . . ." His thoughts focused and the answer came to him as brightly as the ghost itself.

"Wait!" The apprentice stopped. "Water! Water doesn't burn. Maybe, just maybe it would work!"

Desperate, the apprentice reviewed the transmutation spell Durril used when he made lead pieces into gold as a hook for his raree show. It was an act which the apprentice did not fully approve of. The gold lasted only a short time, but transmutation was the only thing Zen could think of to try.

The apprentice concentrated. He made certain adjustments in Durril's spell. He would transmute the fiery specter to water.

Arpad Zen took up a position opposite the spinning ghost. He began the spell. He felt the tingle of the magics crawl along his skin like furry caterpillars. Something was happening. The apprentice carefully worked the spell, emphasizing the changes he had made. He finished it and waited.

At first nothing happened. Then the room was filled with a loud hissing, as if hot metal had been dropped into ice. Rapidly, a warm mist surrounded him.

The burning ghost was gone!

Zen's knees buckled and he slid to the floor, his strength gone from the exertion.

"Bless you." A disembodied voice echoed out of the mist. "Thank you for your kindness," it sobbed. "Even this brief instant of relief can never be repaid."

A bright flare of orange caused Zen to throw up his arm to protect his eyes. Once again the accursed spirit twirled in the center of the room, burning brightly, calling its lonely pain to the winds. Within moments it had blinked out again, turned into mist.

Zen watched in disbelief as the damned ghost changed forms back and forth between fire and mist. This odd shifting of shapes was the best the apprentice could do, and he had no idea how he had accomplished it.

Tukker came through the hatch in the floor into the mist-filled room.

"What are you up to, apprentice? Is he gone?" the tiny man demanded.

"Not exactly," Zen answered. "All I could do is make him blink," he said ruefully.

"Blink?"

"Yes," the miserable apprentice said. "You might say he blinks. I had no spells that would effect an exorcism, so I attempted a transmutation spell. I tried to change him from fire to water, thinking that he wouldn't give off light. That is what you wanted, isn't it?" Arpad Zen babbled. He saw the salvor's wrath mounting at the spell's failure.

"But it didn't exactly work. I mean, I did transmute him, but he doesn't stay transmuted."

At that moment the flame-shrouded ghost reverted to his cursed state of burning, brilliantly lighting the room, his horrible moan assaulting their ears.

". . . 'ware . . . beware . . ."

"See, that's what I mean," the confused apprentice shouted over the wail as he pointed to the whirling, fiery specter. "Now watch, he will change again."

Within moments, the room again filled with mist and the muted quiet fog brought.

"This ain't what I told you to do," Tukker growled at Zen. "You worthless piece of fish gut!"

The wiry little pirate yanked Zen off the floor with a grip like a steel trap and tossed him down the stairs. Rapidly, the wrecker followed the apprentice, a murderous glint in his cold blue eyes.

With a deft roll, Zen came to his feet, crouched and ready for the man's attack. The training Durril had provided his apprentice had

not been solely in magic. As Tukker lunged for
him, Zen stepped aside. With his fingertips he
helped his assailant into the wall.

Although stunned, Tukker recovered quickly
and drew his knife.

"Now you've bought it good and proper, laddie buck. I will have your heart for that . . ."

This time Tukker was more cautious in his
approach. The wrecker feinted with his knife.
Zen shifted but caught himself in time to de-
flect the blade with an unlighted lantern he had
grabbed from a wall hanger.

The two men danced about one another, testing and probing for openings. Tukker was quick
but Zen had been well trained. The apprentice
feinted to his left, then shot forward, knocking
Tukker off his feet.

The wrecker moved like a cat. He rolled, gaining purchase enough to lunge unexpectedly at
Zen. All the apprentice could do to avoid the
sharp knife was to clumsily stumble backward.

"I have you now, laddie," Tukker crowed as
he charged toward Arpad Zen.

Not wasting any breath, Zen crouched to meet
the charge. He deflected the knife with the lantern and threw himself headlong into his foe,
knocking the breath out of the little man as they
toppled onto the floor. Unexpectedly, Tukker
wriggled out of Zen's hold like a slippery eel,
knocking the lantern from the apprentice's
hands. Arpad Zen found himself once more on
the defensive as he backed away from the agile
little man.

The combatants were interrupted by Hammultun, the pudgy wrecker whose ears produced stones in Zen's sleight-of-hand trick.

"Tuk, come quick! We've got a haul. That light is confusin' them merchanters. Two of 'em has piled up on the reef!"

"A lucky break for you, wizard's apprentice," Tukker spat at Zen. "You have your life . . . for the moment." He rushed down the spiral stairs to reach the windswept headlands.

Tukker and Hammultun got out their boats and began the night's grisly work. Zen was left tied to a stake in their hideout. For that he was grateful. The wreckers took no prisoners.

After that night, Zen spent his days under guard as he scavenged for wood and roots on the wild upland around the lighthouse. The wreckers had stopped feeding him and gave him no freedom of movement. His feet were hobbled with a heavy rope. Around his neck he wore a leather collar to which another rope was attached, a leash for his guard to lead him. Although his hands were free, he could do little more than the limited work demanded of him.

He tried some spells against the wreckers but nothing worked. He simply did not know enough to erect a defense against his scraggly persecutors.

Pellas' kingdom—for that is how Zen identified the harsh landscape and rocky coast— Pellas' kingdom was grudging in its bounty. The wind constantly swept over the headland, twisting and distorting the vegetation so that it was a stunted parody of life. The land provided meager firewood and fewer edibles.

Three times more, Tukker forced Zen into the lighthouse tower to confront the damned spirit. Each time, Zen succeeded only in lengthening the time the burning ghost spent as mist. The specter praised Zen for his compassion and mercy. Tukker's crew were delighted at the plunder they reaped because of the now inconstant light. And Arpad Zen's misery grew to despair.

"Morasha is right," he bemoaned to himself as he leaned against the rocky wall of the thieves' den. "I can't do anything right." The words rumbled in the cave.

He wondered where the ogre was, if she had survived. He longed for the companionship of his master, and Durril's protection.

"At least I have relieved the misery of that poor creature in the lighthouse," he consoled himself. "I've never asked his name." Zen paused in surprise.

"But I cannot dissolve him permanently. That would be the kindest deed possible. What I've done for him has caused the deaths of hundreds of good men."

The apprentice sat alone as the wreckers plied their trade along the inhospitable coast. Kept tied to the stake when the robber band did not have a use for him, Zen had ample time to think about his sorry situation.

His fight with Tukker had earned the little man's enduring enmity and spite. Zen constantly watched his step lest he fall afoul of the leader and thereby lose his life.

The strong ropes abraded his ankles and wrists, but there was little Zen could do. Leaving nothing to chance, the wreckers had cleared the area around him, carefully placing the fire and any objects that could be used for cutting out of reach.

Arpad Zen faced the bleakness of his condition. Although Tukker and his unholy gang were now satisfied with his work concerning the burning ghost, there was little else for the apprentice to do. He did not think they would tolerate him much longer. Being a meal for the crabs still did not appeal to him.

"If only Morasha were here." He sighed, wondering what had happened to the ogre familiar.

"I never thought I would say that." Zen managed a laugh as the memory of her scolding tongue lashed at him.

"I would be glad for the sound of her nagging voice," he forlornly admitted to the empty room.

Chapter Five

✤ ✤ ✤

"ALL RIGHT, YOU ectoplasmic mongrels," Durril whispered at the stinging pink eels guarding his cell, "prepare to take a long and peaceful nap."

As the wizard cast his observation spell a second time, he included a bridge to the soporific enchantment. He did not want to alarm the sea nymph by dissolving her bodyguards and thus reveal his reviving powers. Instead, Durril hoped to slip away unnoticed, hiding until he fashioned a plan of action.

Durril did not complete the chants. The squid escort interrupted his conjuring, floating in and grabbing him in an unbreakable grip before carrying him back to the treasure room. The squid deposited him at the foot of the sea nymph's throne.

Sunlight streamed through the water, brightly lighting the hoard twinkling on the bone-white sand. The wizard squinted, trying to focus on the constantly moving and slightly distorted images of the water realm.

In the intense light, Rusalka shone like a jewel throw onto the ocean floor. Her red hair, turned to burnished gold by the sunlight, stroked her pale body gently as it wrapped about her. Momentarily, Durril was bewitched by the sea nymph's exotic, mysterious beauty. He forgot about her craft and menacing power as he gazed on the fullness of her pale breasts pressing against the rainbow-scaled garment that floated on the undersea currents.

Was this the beauty his father had known and never forgotten?

Rusalka's court assembled about her. Durril wondered at the myriad creatures, both real and ectoplasmic, swimming to surround him. They formed a large semicircle before the throne. Arranged in layers, from bottom crawlers to the man-of-war net which floated on the surface of the ocean, the assembly chattered among themselves, apparently uninterested in him or his plight.

Around the perimeter were stationed moray guards, their skin a deeper green reflection of the water. Durril eyed them with more than a little fear. The snakelike morays' bite injected a poison which caused instant paralysis and death. Ranging with the morays were giant ocean centipedes, beings created by the battling wizards of the Spell Wars. Moving slowly about the group, the deep purple centipedes patrolled at several levels. The lazy pace gave the lie to their speed when attacking prey, suffocating it in inky vomit.

"What does Rusalka fear to take such extreme precautions?" Durril wondered to himself.

Rusalka's kingdom boasted a startling variety of beings, real and ghostly. Durril's eye was arrested by a huge lamprey mutated in the wars into a glowing magenta stalker. He was amused by a group of puffer fish occupied in outbluffing one another as they jockeyed for position in the crowd. Intrigued, he looked at them a second time using his observation spell. They appeared to be underwater buffoons; his spell revealed the truth. The puffer fish were deadly, the spines on their swollen bodies pulsating with virulent poisons.

The sea nymph had not detected his minor use of the spell. Risking exposure, but needing the information, Durril quickly scanned the entire assembly. It was a mixture of ectoplasmic beings and physical creatures, most of them death carriers.

"Lords and Ladies of the court," bellowed the herald, a powerful sea centaur. "All hail the Lady Rusalka, Keeper of the Realm."

Rusalka wasted no time as she addressed her retainers.

"Members of this court, I am grateful for your presence today. I have called you to consider matters of grave importance which have imperiled our realm and to pass judgment on the one who has endangered us."

The sea nymph turned to Durril, pronouncing in a loud voice, for all to hear, the accusations against him.

"You are brought here today, master wizard Durril, to stand trial for treachery against this realm."

Durril's thoughts drifted and he lost track of her indictment. Rusalka had donned the crown of her rank as befitted the importance of the meeting. Made of yellow stones which fractured light like a prism, only tingeing each part of the spectrum with a golden hue, the crown held Durril's undivided attention.

The wizard stroked the hem of his jerkin with his right hand. He had lost his kit and his payment from Lord Northdell, but he still had the necklace with its red and blue stones which he had lifted from the vain Lady Kalindi. The sea nymph's crown held the second ingredient he required for casting the Spell Mirror. Because the yellow stones were so potent, only one was needed for the making of the magical device.

"Maybe things aren't so bad," Durril reassured himself. "They just might improve soon."

"How do you plead, master wizard Durril?"

Durril jumped, recalled from his speculations by the pregnant silence surrounding him. Tearing his focus from Rusalka's tantalizing crown, he looked about the assembly, then back to the sea nymph who glared at him.

"How do you plead?" she repeated, irritation like rough sand in her words.

"To what?" Durril had heard little of her pretty speech.

"Did you not hear the charges against you?"

"I admit that I have not, Rusalka. I was so

taken with your beauty that all else faded before me," Durril answered gallantly, executing
a courtly bow.

The court tittered with appreciative laughter
but was immediately silenced by the sea
nymph's seething countenance.

"I shall begin again, wizard Durril. Pray, pay
attention. The charges are most serious."

Without pausing, she continued. "You are
brought to trial today under the charges of theft
and treachery against this realm. How do you
plead?"

"Oh." Durril laughed in dismissal. "Not
guilty, of course."

The court responded once again with muffled
laughter that rippled and gurgled but rapidly
faded as Rusalka began to detail the charges
against the wizard.

She was interrupted again when a venerable
sea turtle swam to rest before her throne. His
leather back sported deep scars, the ravages of
age and adventure. A respectful hush descended over the court.

"My Lady Rusalka," he said in greeting.

"My Lord Chelonia," Rusalka replied, obviously unsettled by the aged reptile's presence.
"You honor us with your presence. We thought
you had forsaken our company for a hermit's
life."

"I could not refuse the call to assembly when
matters of such urgency to the welfare of this
realm were to be discussed." Chelonia said in a
deep voice that boomed and echoed through the
court.

"What may I do for you, Lord Chelonia?" The
sea nymph hurried onward, anxious to dis-

pense with the courtesies due the distinguished lord and get on with the trial.

"Has this man anyone who will defend his actions?"

The sea nymph was clearly upset by the turtle's question. While the sea nymph was occupied, Durril used his observation spell and determined that the venerable old lord was indeed a physical being, although an ancient specimen of his kind. And there was something else about him which Durril could not interpret.

"None," she answered grudgingly.

"Then he must have a champion, Lady Rusalka. With charges bearing weight of such severity, he cannot be left undefended. And he must have a jury. It is our way. The Mother Ocean is equitable to those who strive with her," Lord Chelonia reminded the assembly. "We who inhabit her must act in the same manner."

Infuriated, Rusalka glared at the aged reptile, but the congregation murmured its agreement. She barely held her tongue in check.

"So," Durril said softly, "she does not have complete authority."

"Lord Chelonia," the sea nymph said, a cold smile forming which displayed her even white teeth. "Who in our congregation would be willing to defend such perfidy?"

No one spoke, clearly aware of the sea nymph's hostility.

"I will champion him, Rusalka," the aged lord replied. "I am old and have seen many wonders in my life. I an unafraid of discovering another."

"Very well," Rusalka said angrily.

The court would have its full proceedings. They had not met in convocation for many years, something she had managed to prevent. Now assembled, they would not be denied their entertainment. Durril felt the tense excitement in the undersea denizens.

Rusalka rose and appointed the jurors without discussion with Chelonia. The aged turtle made no comment about the ease with which she found willing jurors. Durril started to protest but Chelonia snapped his powerful beak shut once, silencing any protest.

The assembly relaxed, ready for the show. She chose several harmless fish and a ghostly carp with poisonous fangs for teeth. To Durril's astonishment, Rusalka bypassed the glowing red shark-phantoms to appoint an innocuous flatworm as the last member of the panel.

A reaction of dread among the members of the court alerted Durril to the importance of the sea nymph's final choice. Once again he employed the observation spell, this time on the flatworm. It took much control not to betray his shock at what he saw.

The worm was a poisonous remnant of the Spell Wars. Within Durril's magic sight, it shone a putrescent red. In some ways it was very uncomplicated. That simplicity was dedicated to only one thing: the painful, burning death of whatever came within its treacherous grasp. Worse, the worm was somehow bonded to the sea nymph. She exercised complete control over it.

If she did not like the verdict, Rusalka could

enforce her own decision with lightning speed through the deadly creature.

"Sharpen your ax before you chop," Durril reminded himself. "Rusalka is indeed a sorceress of unlimited talent and potential, untrained though she is. I need to find out everything before acting."

Ignoring this last appointment to the panel, Lord Chelonia took his place in the center of the floor before the court and jury. He nodded to Durril but did not speak. The wizard acknowledged the giant reptile with a feeble smile.

All the formalities now observed, Rusalka opened the arguments by stating the offenses Durril had supposedly committed.

"You see before you, honored Lords and Ladies of this deep realm, some of the treasure hoard this human wizard caused to be scattered from us."

Part of Durril's trade goods were piled before the throne. His heart raced at the sight. He looked them over, hoping to find his magic kit among the exquisite glass and gold work of Loke-Bor. It was not there. Although he saw some armor, beautifully inlaid with filigreed stonework, no swords accompanied it. Durril wondered if they had been carefully left out of the exhibits.

"Consider the unrepentant defiance of the wizard Durril," Rusalka continued. "He dared challenge my vortex and the storm. This opposition we cannot tolerate," the sea nymph cried, many in the court bobbing up and down in agreement. "It is our right to take what comes to us on the water."

Ghosts of the *Pitcairn*'s crew were herded into the arena by two ectoplasmic sea serpents with cherubic human faces. When they snapped at the disoriented specters, the serpents bared glowing green poisonous fangs capable of inflicting agony on any being, physical or spectral. The ghostly mutinous crew were penned to the left of Rusalka's high throne. Already, the sea had begun its transformation on them. They glowed pearlescent where their ectoplasmic surface met the lapping, briny water.

"We increase our numbers," Rusalka said proudly as she indicated the ghost sailors, "as well as our wealth." She stood and thrust her arms high over her head. Durril found himself mesmerized anew by her exotic beauty.

"I use my powers in your service to accomplish these ends. The vortex and the storm are mine to control for your benefit."

Her prideful statements broke the wizard's reverie. Durril furtively cast another observation spell. It confirmed the ghosts of the mutinous crew. He shifted his spell to the sea nymph herself. If she noticed his action she did not acknowledge it.

She was a physical being, although she shimmered like a wraith because of the water's constant movement. Rusalka glared at him, the eerie light reflecting from the deep amber of her eyes, a shade darker than the powerful stones in her crown. She turned away, back to the business of the trial.

The wizard wondered if the sea nymph's embrace would be as warm as the blood she stirred in him. He shook himself. What an enchantress she was! He had never understood his father's attraction to the undersea world before now.

"If he had only prevented the taking of treasure, the wizard Durril's crimes would have merited our severe punishment." Rusalka spoke once more, forcing Durril to pay attention to the charges. "But he has done more to harm us. Durril's treachery reaches deeper than mere opposition to our rights. His treachery causes a great wounding of this kingdom which is beyond repair."

The assembled host broke out in puzzled murmurs, speculations about the wizard's heinous crimes. The sea nymph waited for them to fall silent, knowing that she had their concern with her now.

Durril himself wondered what accusation Rusalka would make. Lord Chelonia rested patiently, flippers moving slowly, waiting for Rusalka to conclude her accusations.

"The *master* wizard Durril is the repository of knowledge which by ancient right belongs to me," Rusalka said. She hurried into a full explanation, the heat of her desire for revenge stoking fire into her steel-edged words.

"Keeral, his accursed father, enchanted my sister, the sea nymph Vila. He married Vila and made her teach him the whole of her wisdom. As you are well aware, it is our custom for such lore to be passed from the eldest to the youngest in our sisterhood. What Keeral received from Vila was by right and tradition mine." Rusalka's face hardened as memory of her sister's love for a human drowned out all reason.

"Vila died in defense of her lover. He in turn deserted our realm, taking with him my inheritance. It is Durril who now holds our ancient lore, the power of our realm. He has stolen my birthright from me—he has taken from you your glory." She spun and faced the jury.

"My loyal retainers, need I say more?" Seeing that she did, Rusalka hurried on, her wrath burning in every word. "Consider the harm Durril has caused us and render your verdict, which *must* be a long and painful death!"

With satisfaction, Rusalka sat on the throne as the assembly erupted into loud debate. She smiled and looked triumphantly at Durril, who betrayed no emotion in the midst of the clamor.

"So that was it," Durril muttered. "She is cunning, a talented sorceress. But there is a cold streak in her, like those power-hungry wizards who ruined the world during the Spell Wars. What would she do with unlimited knowledge and no checks upon her power?"

Durril paid close attention to the proceedings and to Rusalka. The sea nymph was quite capable of launching the worm if things did not go her way.

"My Lady Rusalka," Chelonia began as the host focused on him. "I speak as champion for the wizard Durril who stands accused of warring with this kingdom in the person of its sea nymph, of theft, and of complete and total treachery. I submit to you that these charges are baseless!"

Durril saw that age and experience did not fear Rusalka, as Lord Chelonia conducted his defense. He was indeed lucky to have such an advocate in this forum. The audience's attention was riveted to Lord Chelonia and his challenge to their ruler.

"The accused acted in opposition to you, Rusalka, only in response to his basic nature. He acted in defense of what he saw as his own property. Do we not all behave in the same manner when our territory is invaded?"

The assembled court nodded agreement with the old lord, some more aggressive members giving scattered shouts of "Hear, hear!" The jurors remained noncommittal.

"You have secured his treasure, Rusalka. It lies before you. Even as we speak, your retainers search for the remainder. I am confident that it will all be gathered to you. What you have experienced is only a minor inconvenience. You cannot accuse him of stealing this treasure since you possess it! The Mother Ocean allows those who travel on her to strive with her for their life and possessions. If they are skillful, the travelers retain both. This is the way of our world. *You* cannot reverse it," he reminded the sea nymph. "Durril was an honorable opponent, but you have won his treasure!"

"I will dismiss that charge, venerable Chelonia. I will dismiss the charge of warring on this realm," the sea nymph interjected impatiently, chafing at the blatant challenge to her authority presented by the ancient turtle.

"The crime which is the only question here is the theft of my birthright and the hampering of this kingdom because of it," she said, showing the fullness of her anger.

"I submit, Rusalka," Lord Chelonia said, confronting the sea nymph once more, "that your concern about harm to our realm is really only what you see as impediment to your personal power."

So he sees it, too, Durril thought, grateful to the old turtle for bringing out the truth of the matter.

No one in the congregation uttered a sound. Even the guards had stopped their patrolling, taken aback by the open conflict between the sea nymph and her distinguished retainer.

Before Rusalka could respond, Chelonia continued. "I further submit that the wizard Durril is guiltless of that charge. Durril could not take your birthright. The father's actions are not visited upon the son. We all choose our own destinies!" the venerable lord thundered.

Raising his flipper he cautioned Rusalka to silence.

"I knew the sea nymph Vila, and I knew her husband, the master wizard Keeral. I testify now to this court that Vila would never have initiated you into her knowledge, even if she had not married."

"That is not so, Chelonia," Rusalka denied.

"It is true, Rusalka. Vila worried over your seeking of power, and about what you might do if you became a master of the lore. She planned to withhold the greater lore from you, fearing that you might do much damage with only elementary knowledge.

"Vila had chosen to spread her knowledge among us all. She dreamed of establishing for us a parliament of powers working for our mutual good. She had already begun the process at the time of her death. She made Keeral promise that if anything happened to her, he would take the wisdom out of the sea so that it could not be corrupted."

"Lies!" the sea nymph shrieked.

"Not lies, Rusalka. The truth!" Chelonia rose in the water until he floated level with her throne. "Alas, Vila sacrificed herself in defense of this realm before she could accomplish the whole of her goal. She was convinced that only through the sharing of power could we defeat the great evil which stalks us." Chelonia spun around to face the jury. One huge gimlet eye blinked in their direction, but he directed the full force of his oratory toward the assembled multitudes.

"I am here today to speak to that threat, Rusalka. I will not allow you to indulge yourself with this sham when the realm faces total annihilation!"

Pandemonium erupted among the assembly as individuals and groups debated Chelonia's challenge.

"Enough, you doddering old fool!" Rusalka screamed. "I mean to have his life! Worm!" the sea nymph commanded, pointing at the deadly flatworm.

Durril was ready. He had fixed the observation spell on the hideous worm and began the most potent exorcism chant in his arsenal of spells.

Rusalka did not complete the command. The assembled company succumbed to panic, their alarmed cries echoing about the grotto. Engrossed in the drama unfolding in the court before them, the guards had neglected their duties.

"The Vodyanoi! The Vodyanoi!" a glowing red shark shrieked as it sped away.

Immediately, the pink eels formed a barrier around the sea nymph as they began a deafening thrum. For a moment, Durril was forgotten. In the confusion, he broke concentration and lost the thread of the spell he had begun to weave. All hope of exorcising the worm vanished when a luminescent squid grabbed him, dragging him toward Rusalka's throne as the court scattered in fear of its life. Only the Lord Chelonia remained.

Then the Vodyanoi struck.

Chapter Six
✤ ✤ ✤

"KILL THE OGRE! Kill the ogre!"

The rhythmical chant pounded throughout the darkening woods. It beat at the familiar like the madness of drums.

Morasha ran, tripping over fallen debris in the scrubby forest, her thick skin scratched and torn by thorny trees and bushes. She dared not stop to tend the minor lacerations. The sound of the hunting chant followed her through the woods, hounding her as she ran for her life.

Earlier, she had stumbled into a tiny village at the edge of the forest. Her first day on the island had taught her to avoid any settlement, but this one had been hidden close against the trees. Before she saw the danger, peasants rushed forth to attack her. The familiar had been chased sporadically but never as fiercely as this.

Morasha heard the pursuers thrashing about close behind, their bloodthirsty cries sounding like a pack of baying hounds in the cool, dense evening air.

"This way, it went this way! See, there are marks of its gore!"

"Hurry! The monster is wounded!"

"We'll sacrifice no more babies to the horror!" a woman's voice screeched.

Laboring onward, Morasha crashed through the underbrush without any attempt at stealth. She had ripped a gash in her foot and walked with difficulty. The once strong ogre body carried multiple wounds which refused to heal. The exorcism that had caused this body to become physical had weakened it. The familiar feared that the body would be useless soon. But she had no time for such speculation now. Morasha ran as fast as she could away from the hidden village and its murderous tenants.

Looking back, she saw flashes of light through the trees.

"Torches!" Morasha gasped, running harder. She heard the crackle of dry wood as it caught fire; the scent of the burning forest assaulted her nostrils.

"Head it off," came a voice on her right. Loud yells of agreement followed the order.

More torches flickered, still behind but circling to flank her. Then orange flame licked hungrily at the undergrowth, rapidly outracing her, forcing her to turn left.

Morasha's chest hurt from the strain of running. Her legs quivered beneath her. She dared not face her pursuers; there were too many of them and she lacked the strength to fight them. All she could do was blunder headlong through the terrible forest and hope to outdistance the hunters.

She quickly saw that hope fade. The fire traveled much faster than the villagers. It vaulted through the dry forest with a will of its own. Morasha felt the intense heat on her back as she ran. Smoke and ash assaulted her nostrils.

The vengeful cries had faded to be replaced by the roar of the fire as the woods exploded in flame. It almost surrounded her. Desperate, Morasha beat her way forward.

She ran blindly through the night and the choking smoke, away from the militant villagers. She pushed into a thicket of bracken, causing more damage to her already abraded skin. At last, unbelievably, she was free of the tormenting forest which snapped and whined in its fiery death throes behind her.

Still running hard, ungainly in her stride because of her injuries, Morasha bolted across the open moor and flung herself headlong into the protecting embrace of a stand of boulders. Panting, the familiar let her ogre body rest, trying to blend into the mottled rock under the probing starlight.

She looked back at the burning woods, her eyes still smarting from the smoke, her chest heaving. No one came for her from the inferno.

"Arpad Zen would have to get himself lost," she gasped in complaint to the shielding rocks.

"When I get my hands on him, I shall wring his scrawny neck," she vowed.

Her foot ached. The cut had gone deep. Dark slime seeped through where the wound had swollen and crusted over. Her whole body was a mass of scratches and bruises. Moving sent lances of pain throughout her once powerful body.

"Damn that apprentice!" the familiar cursed, blaming him still for her present troubles.

She lay in the security of the defending boulders and rested, unable to move. Eyes closed and head aching, Morasha wondered if her hunt for Zen was worth further effort. She had searched toward the lighthouse as she zigzagged across the countryside, taking advantage of what cover she found. Mostly she had traveled at night. The damaged body had slowed her. Then her foul luck had bitten her again. Something had gone awry with the lighthouse beacon, causing her to lose her way.

Forced to travel inland because of a rough jumble of rock which scarred the island, Morasha had run afoul of the villagers. If she had possessed Durril's magical sight and experience, the familiar would have known the sharp, broken earth to be the result of a contest of powers during the wars.

All she knew was that the rough passage gave no sure purchase to the foot traveler. She had traveled inland attempting to skirt it—and this had brought forth the pack of villagers.

Morasha again checked the forest. It continued to burn with undiminished ferocity, but no one came for her. She carefully surveyed the open countryside toward the sea. Morasha listened for any sound which would indicate the chase. Only the muffled roar of the fire and the wind whistling over the desolate moor reached her ears. A nightbird called its lonely song high overhead.

Along the top of a ridge some distance away, she spotted the outline of another sheltering outcrop of rocks. The familiar made them her destination. As quickly as her wounded foot and injured body would allow, Morasha limped across the uneven moor. She traveled hunched over, trying to camouflage herself by keeping close to the earth.

"I'll find him," she muttered under her breath as she labored up the long incline leading to the ridge. "He will pay for this if it's the last thing I do. If I had that strong, fine hawk's body now, I wouldn't be the victim of these indignities. I'd rip his eyes out with my talons!"

Morasha gained the ridge. She took refuge once more within boulders as she spied out the open land on the other side. Her heart sank. Below her was a crossroads and another village.

All seemed peaceful but she dared not chance discovery. She hunkered down amid the rocky cover, grateful for a cooling sea breeze. Her ogre body had produced a strong, pungent odor since her dousing in the ocean. Furtively she watched the village until the last candles were snuffed out for the night. She waited.

Very late in the night, she made her way along the ridge, working toward the confusing beacon in the lighthouse. The lay of the land forced her downward toward the road, her only cover infrequent plots of scrub cedar. If she crossed the road and gained the woods on the other side, she might be safe.

Morasha sat and waited, immobile next to a clump of cedar not half a league from the village. She strained to distinguish the sounds of the night. Her eyes ached as they probed the dark countryside. Every slight sound, every shifting shadow, every unusual night scent, held terror for her. At last, unable to stand the uncertainty longer, she bolted down the incline and pounded across the rutted dirt road, making for the safety of the woods.

A night scavenger screamed, causing her to cry out, adding her protest to the stillness of the night.

She flung herself into the underbrush. Unable to stand, Morasha crawled into the woods, further scraping her body. Unseen animals gave voice over this intrusion and ran. Finally she could go no farther. Hugging the base of a gigantic oak, the familiar listened for pursuers. She heard only the night wind through the trees and the scampering of small animals frightened by her noisy passage. Tears tumbled from her eyes. She sat trembling in the dark, her will as broken as her body.

Exhausted, Morasha slept, awakening to the brilliant noon light filtering through the dense canopy of rustling dry leaves above her. Startled that she had slept so long, she sat up, listening again for the chase.

Her foot throbbed. In the midday light she saw its sickening green color as well as the swollen flesh. The patchwork of cuts, bruises, and scrapes covering the rest of her clumsy body looked as bad as they felt. The hair on her back was singed. She shivered at how close the fire had come to claiming her. This simple involuntary shudder sent pain throughout her body. The injured foot again commanded the focus of her attention.

"Something must be caught in the wound," she thought. When she touched the festering gash, the pain was too sharp for her to continue probing.

Struggling to her feet, she started making her slow way through the forest, getting her bearings from the wind direction. If she could reach the beach once again, traveling along the rugged coastline might be easier than fighting the entangling woods and the bloodthirsty villagers.

Dizziness overcame Morasha after a few minutes' travel. She stopped, waiting for the world to quit spinning. When the ogre body became fully physical, it also became subject to the needs of flesh. Morasha was hungry. What was she to do?

Searching the undergrowth for anything edible, she eventually found a few overripe berries. A clump of mushrooms gave a second mouthful. It wasn't enough, but her head cleared as she continued walking, dragging her swollen foot through the autumn leaves scattered about the forest floor.

In the early afternoon, Morasha reached the edge of the woods but did not leave them. The forest bordered cultivated fields. A team of men and oxen worked at the far side of the lot, making their methodical way to the end of the furrow, then returning in Morasha's direction. Morasha shrank back into the cover of the undergrowth as the nervous team came closer. The plowman turned without sounding an alarm, mixing the fresh manure with the chaff of his wheat crop in preparation for next year's planting.

Fading into the forest, Morasha skirted the edge of the field, trying to cut across the woods paralleling it. By evening she was hungry again. She had found a small stream and some more late berries. Her wounded foot ached.

"There is nothing to do but open it," she said aloud, steeling herself for what had to be done.

Morasha settled her foot on clean leaves she had collected. She stifled her cry of pain. Then she washed the foot with cool water. After the throbbing eased, she made a bed out of more of the sweet-smelling foliage. For the first time since washing onto the island, Morasha slept peacefully through the night.

She awakened at first light, hungry again. A family of rabbits were drinking at the stream, the young roughhousing with one another. At her approach, they stopped and stared at her, ears up and pink noses twitching.

"I'll find my food elsewhere," she assured them.

As the rabbits scattered into the undergrowth, Morasha foraged once again, this time finding a bountiful crop of mushrooms by a hollow log. By mid-morning she had returned to the edge of the field. No one was in sight.

Her injured foot, although still tender, had improved. Morasha decided to chance it. She bolted from the forest cover and ran for the stone fencing which enclosed the field on the seaward side. On the other side, she was once

again in the wild country of moors and up-
thrusting rocks.

Throughout the day, Morasha made her way
across the uninhabited land, carefully planning
her forays from shelter to shelter until she
came to a ridge near the lighthouse. Below her
stretched a moor painted with the last bloodred
rays of the setting sun. Their rusty light covered the world with a sickly hue, making it difficult to distinguish features in the landscape.

Movement across the field caught her. An animal staked there foraged about in the earth for
its supper. The familiar stayed put. A copse of
wind-twisted trees hid her well. A staked animal meant that its owner would be nearby.
Confirming her suspicions, Morasha saw a light
bobbing along the edge of the headland.

"Obviously a lantern carried by the animal's
owner," she said, instinctively sinking farther
into the dark trees.

But Morasha's curiosity was aroused. Who
would stake an animal on this barren headland? She peeked between the trunks of two
trees to see the bright yellow light from the lantern fall across the apprentice's troubled face.

"Arpad Zen!" Morasha said in astonishment.

The familiar watched as Zen was dragged behind his keeper. She could not make out the
words, but the tone of the instructions shouted
at the apprentice was clear.

"What has he gotten himself into now?" Morasha said in frustration, preparing to follow.

She waited until the lantern's light sank below the cliff edge, then made her way across the
open ground.

The tricky trail to the beach made for slow progress. Morasha watched the two men and the bobbing lantern until they reached the bottom. Then she began her descent. The familiar reached the foot of the trail in time to see the bobbing light disappear as if it had been swallowed by the earth.

"A cave. There must be a cave," she told herself as she headed after Arpad Zen.

Shouts of rough merriment led Morasha to the wrecker's hideout. She worked her way to the downwind side of it, taking no chances that the distinctive smell of her ogre body would betray her. What she saw after she crept up to the encampment distressed her.

A miserable Arpad Zen was staked in the center of the rough gang. He was gamely attempting to juggle some empty bottles while the unsavory crew taunted him, purposely prodding or tripping him to cause misfortune.

There were at least forty of them—too many for Morasha to attack. Even in the ogre form, she could not match so many cutthroats in direct combat. Worse, her strength faded quickly.

"Ow!" the apprentice cried as the wreckers pelted him with small, sharp stones they had forced him to gather. He danced about the menacing circle, unable to escape their punishments. The company was spurred on by his howls and protests.

"Are ye hungry?" a swarthy brute teased, offering a greasy joint to Zen.

Morasha knew the apprentice needed food. He looked starved. It was obvious that he wanted to accept the offered meat but was

caught between his hunger and the cruelty of
the wrecker.

"You can have it, wizard's fool, if you'll beg,"
the man taunted. "Say please. I might let ye kiss
my boot and . . . eat this!" He held the roast
haunch just beyond Zen's weak grasp.

Drunken laughter filled the air as several
members of the gang echoed their mate's instructions.

Ashamed, but famished, Arpad Zen reached
toward his dark tormenter.

"Please," the apprentice croaked.

"On your knees!" the wrecker ordered.

"Please," Zen said a second time as he sank
to his knees on the sandy floor.

"Why sure." The wrecker laughed. "I'm such
a fine fellow, I won't even make ye lick my
boots." He stepped back from where Zen
crouched, hands and knees on the floor of the
cave. "Fetch!"

He threw the joint across the circle where it
landed in the sand just at the end of Zen's
tether. The apprentice chased after it, his need
for food overcoming his pride.

Another wrecker retrieved the gristly meat
before Zen could reach it and tossed it back
across the circle. Crying, the apprentice pur-
sued the elusive joint once again to the hilarity
of the cruel lot.

Tukker interrupted the game. "Give it to
him!" the little man ordered. "We have work to
do."

Ignoring Zen, the wrecker crew clustered
about Tukker as he laid out plans for their next
job. Stealthily, Zen retrieved the sand-covered
joint, still afraid someone would snatch it from

him. He gnawed at it like a starving dog having been thrown a bone.

Morasha, who had witnessed the whole unhappy scene, fretted in her hidden nook.

"Even *he* doesn't deserve this," she said, forgetting to berate the apprentice for his shortcomings. "I must free him."

More like her old self, she continued. "He can't save himself, of course. He has to leave it to me after afflicting me with this weakening body."

Grumbling quietly, the familiar carefully made her way back to the safety of the wild headland. There she set about devising a plan to free the troublesome apprentice from the hands of the tormenting gang.

"It should be easy enough to get my hands on him tomorrow," she said to herself, making a nest under the twisted trees that had been her previous refuge. "If they stake him out in the field again, I'll be able to get him away easy enough."

But Arpad Zen was not brought to the field the next day. No one came to the desolate moor. Morasha waited and watched all day until evening when hunger forced her to leave her hideout.

"What's he done now to hinder my rescue plan?" She growled angrily at the roots she had uncovered. "He just can't do anything right!"

Morasha bit into a root, gnawing at it in her frustration. The food did nothing to relieve her worry.

The next evening, villagers came to the moor.

Chapter Seven
✤ ✤ ✤

SWEAT POURED DOWN Arpad Zen's grimy face. His breath came in shallow gasps, and he trembled from the exertion. Although weak from hunger, the apprentice kept chanting his spell.

Locked in the beacon room of the lighthouse since early morning, he tried to dissolve the cursed specter.

Nothing worked except the transmutation spell. Zen again prolonged the mist stage of the ghost's transformation—but that was still the best he could do.

Tired, his constant hunger gnawing at him, he ended the ritual, collapsing onto the floor to rest.

"Better to face a thousand swords head-on than to get a single knife in the back," he mumbled to himself, remembering one of his master's maxims.

Tukker had promised execution if the ghost was not exorcised completely.

The heavy warm mist suffocated Zen. Pulling himself up, the apprentice wizard leaned over the rail encircling the room. He walked to the landward side, preferring the desolation of the headland to the view of sea and the island's treacherous coast. Too many men had died there because of his ineptitude.

Storm clouds darkened the horizon, sullen gray in the waning sunlight. The heavily scented moor below was touched with golden-red light, as if burnished with blood. From the lighthouse tower, the apprentice could see the full length of the distant ridge separating the headland from the fields and forests beyond. He stared out listlessly at the peaceful provincial setting, exhausted by his labors and cruel imprisonment.

Something moved along the ridge, scuttling between clumps of trees and outcroppings of rock. Zen studied it, straining to see what moved in the lonely world spread out below him.

"Morasha!" he exclaimed, hardly believing his eyes. The ogre's ungainly form was unmistakable, but he rubbed his tired eyes and looked again. He had not been deceived by some quirk of sunlight.

"Morasha! Morasha!" he called, waving his arms.

The distance was too great for him to be heard or seen.

"Morasha!" he said, sobbing quietly to himself. The ogre familiar was alive. He hadn't killed her again. And she was near the lighthouse. Maybe there was a chance he could get to her!

Zen's spirits revived. "Not yet, Tukker," he spat, looking about the room for a weapon. "You can't have me just yet!"

The only things handy were the water buckets. Zen hefted one a few inches above the floor, then dropped it. The bucket was heavy enough to harm a man coming through the hatch into the room.

The burning ghost blinked briefly into its fiery state. Just as rapidly it changed back to warm mist. Zen chanted again, strengthening the hold of the mist form on the miserable specter. Then the apprentice lined up four buckets by the trap door and waited as night descended. He didn't wait long.

"Wizard's fool," the swarthy man shouted as he unbolted the door. It swung downward, revealing the golden glow of a lantern. Zen remained frozen to his spot, ready with bucket in hand.

"Wizard's fool!" his cruel tormenter called again, angry. Still the apprentice did not answer.

"By Croy and all his scurvy minions," the wrecker cursed. "Has that fool of an apprentice gone and jumped off the tower?"

Zen clutched the bucket until his fingers hurt. He dared not act too soon. He had to do this right the first time—or die.

"Apprentice!" The command came sharp, demanding.

Muttering additional curses, the swarthy wrecker started up the stairway. Just as his head reached the opening, Zen slammed the water bucket down onto it. The heavy wooden bucket broke apart as Zen's tormenter fell back down the stairs, unconscious before he hit the landing.

Cautiously, the apprentice peered through the opening. No one else was in the room below. Tukker had sent only one wrecker after him. Gingerly, Zen eased down the steps, wary of what he would find waiting for him.

With a deft movement he removed the fallen man's knife and scabbard. He considered slitting the man's throat with his own knife. It was only fitting after the torment he had given. Zen had no stomach for such bloodthirsty murder, however. He gagged the wrecker with a sleeve torn from his own shirt and bound his hands with the other one.

He stood over the dark, disgusting man, knife in hand, then sheathed it.

"There has been too much killing," he said.

Arpad Zen doused the lantern and waited for his eyes to adjust to the dark.

"Set running lights fore and aft."

"Aye, aye, sir. Set running lights fore and aft," the boatswain repeated.

Men scuttled about the decks to obey the order. They attached long poles with lighted lanterns to the shallow draft vessel in which they rode. In the dark of night, the ship would appear longer and higher than it really was. Its running lights now carried the pattern of a merchanter.

"Battle stations."

The command echoed down the deck as the crew responded, each man taking up his equipment and reporting to his assigned station.

"All crew members at battle stations, sir," the boatswain reported.

The ship swiftly approached the narrow straits where so many merchanters had met their death on the rocky, barren reef. Under the command of Captain Waine of the Wonnean Merchant Marine, the shipload of assault troops made ready to effect a landing on the wrecker's beach. All were battle-hardened veterans of numerous other assaults.

The great merchants of Wonne had had

enough of the wreckers' interference with trade ships bound for their port. Too many good cargoes had been lost, too many credits kept from their accounts. Some saw in their efforts to protect their material interests a chance for reunification, an unfulfilled dream since the Wars. But the populace of the Plenn Archipelagoes were suspicious of power concentrated in the hands of the few. The contentious wizards of the Spell Wars had taught them well the disadvantage of such might.

In spite of opposition, the Wonnean Merchant Marine had been formed. The leaders of the trading city considered this a service to customers when piracy and wrecking became the livelihood of otherwise uncontrollable elements.

As the marines neared the uninviting shoreline, the lookout spied several decoy lights.

"They surely give a muddled signal, Captain. You can't be sure what shore you're approaching, and the charts will do you no good here. They are clever devils," the chief officer said.

The confusion created by the odd lights confirmed that the marines had found their target. Only once during their approach did the great lighthouse beacon show itself. It burned bright for an instant and then faded into the dark night.

Each member of the thirty-two-man company carried an inflated pig's bladder as a float. Many could not swim, as was typical of the superstitious sea-going men of the Plenn Archipelagoes. Most had a mole tattooed on one ankle and an ox on the other as a ward against the Mother Ocean's greed for companions.

Weapons ready, a dummy tied to each pack, the crew arranged itself into squads of eight men each. Each marine wore light armor of boiled leather impregnated with oil. They manned the rails of the sleek, fast ship, ready to take to the sea when it broke apart on the reef.

Lassrin paced the deck, anxious to be on the scent. The ghostly bloodhound, a more reasonable remnant of the Spell Wars, had been recruited into the merchant marine service along with his living partner, Johee. The lad and his unusual spectral dog had fallen in together after Johee was orphaned.

The sniffer ghost never lost a scent once it locked on, and it could not be confused by overlaying scents. It fought with the ferocity of undivided loyalty in its silent, deadly attacks. Bonded with Johee, Lassrin was the indispensable weapon of the elite amphibious force from Wonne.

"Steady as she goes," Captain Waine ordered as the ship approached the treacherous reef.

The troops heard the roar of pounding water beating against unmoving stones. Each trooper made his private devotions, his blood running high in preparation for the imminent invasion. Even Captain Waine was unsure of what they would find ashore. Their orders were straightforward: take the coastline and hold it until a permanent contingent arrived. Never again would trading vessels be lured from their markets along this shore. As always when dealing with wreckers, Waine would take no prisoners this night.

Unhesitatingly, the helmsman steered into the

rocks opposite the lighthouse. With a great shuddering crack, the troopship broke asunder, propelling its deadly cargo into the churning water. The night air filled with terrified yells and cries for help as the well-disciplined squads made for shore, floating over the obstructing reef under cover of the dark and the stormcast sky.

Lassrin paddled beside Johee, man and ghost dog traveling with the lightest gear, making it hard for any on shore to see them. The pair of hunters achieved the beach well ahead of the other troops.

"Lassrin, search and locate! That's a good boy!" Johee said.

The ghostly bloodhound bounded away down the coast, its keen senses alert for any menace to its master and the troops.

Johee set up a base camp in a handy rock notch against the cliff and waited. Occasionally he gave a soft, long whistle, the sound of a flying nightbird, so that his confederates could easily locate the headquarters he'd established.

As the remaining troops hit the beach, they cut loose their dummies, leaving them to litter the shore, decoy bodies waiting for the wreckers.

The marines hurried toward Johee's whistle. Those who could throw their voices maintained a chorus of moans, a feint to lure their prey into the carefully laid trap.

As each squad leader reached the headquarters, he gathered his men and started along the coast to establish a skirmish line with its back to the sheer cliff and its front to the pounding surf.

Not all the marines made the landing. One contingent held back in the water, biding its time, the second claw of a pincer destined to close on the unsavory group who dared oppose the merchants and bankers of Wonne.

Lassrin bounded into Johee's arms, flushed with pride and success in his mission. He emitted soft woofs and grunts which only his master could understand, although the inventive bloodhound had been working out a series of semaphore-type signals with his ears. From Lassrin's point of view, the one called Waine had potential to understand the signals, but he was slow-witted and kept getting confused.

"They are to the north of us, Captain," Johee reported, "about half a mile. There are between thirty-five and forty of them, all heavily armed."

Once again, Lassrin spoke. This time low growls sounded among the soft barks.

"They are all armed, sir," Johee interpreted. "Lassrin says they smell bad, that we should be careful."

"Right," Waine responded. "A job well done, Lassrin. Johee, give the signal to hold. We want the scum to walk into our little welcoming party without any suspicions. I'll have the ears of anyone moving before I give the order."

Johee whistled a series of bird calls designed to convey the captain's wishes. The marines waited.

"All right men, to work!" Tukker laughed as he ordered the wreckers to range the beach.

The jovial gang came at a trot toward the decoys, ready to dispatch any shipwrecked crewman who still lived and relieve him of his worldly goods. Trevoor struck first. His sharp sword slashed through an exposed neck—a small flood of sea-dampened sawdust was his only reward.

"What the—? Tuk, Tuk, come quick," Trevoor called. "Somethin's bad wrong here."

Captain Waine heard the confusion and fear in the wrecker's voice. The pounding of boots against the wet sand told of other pirates joining him.

"Now, Johee, sound the attack," Waine ordered.

The scream of a sea eagle pierced the gloomy night. Blood-curdling yells quickly followed. Lassrin let out a long, mournful bay, calling his charge into the fray.

Panic gripped the wrecking crew, but Tukker rallied them.

"Stand and fight, you scurvy bunch of good-for-nothin's or you'll have to deal with me," he shouted at his confused, frightened gang of wreckers.

Trevoor took one flank of the wreckers' line, holding them to the fight, while Tukker anchored the other. The gang members set their backs to the sea just in time to meet the marine charge. Chaos erupted on the beach.

Lassrin blasted through the wreckers like storm wind. He nipped at their heels and slashed calves, creating havoc among the wreckers. All the while, the translucent, ghostly hound kept sounding his horrifying bay.

Hand to hand, the desperate wreckers contended with the disciplined Wonnean marines. Confused, they hacked and slashed at one another in the surf. Tukker fought his own men as hard as he did the marines.

"You fools! They are comin' at us from the cliffs! Turn your backs to the sea and fight them head-on! Don't go killin' each other. After them. *After them!*"

The pirates rallied. One wrecker grabbed Johee by the hair from behind and wrestled the slight lad to the sand. As he moved to slash the boy's throat, Lassrin felled him.

The specter bloodhound hit the offending wrecker, knocking him backward. With one swift snap, the ghostly dog ripped out the man's throat, leaving him to gurgle the last of his life into the salty tide washing over him.

Captain Waine got Trevoor by the ears and rammed the weaselly man's head into his swiftly rising knee. Then he snapped his neck, discarding his body on the sand. Waine moved on to help his lieutenant, who held two swordsmen at bay. With Trevoor's death, the end of the wreckers' line wavered and started to run.

Flight did not come easily. They were cut off from escape by the assault of the contingent from the sea.

The wet squad closed on the wreckers' broken line with spine-tingling battle cries, further panicking the now-surrounded gang. One by one the marines methodically dispatched the unsavory crew.

Tukker fought with the ferocity of a trapped animal. The swift little man ducked under the guard of two marines coming for him, deftly gutting them with upward thrusts of his knives. They fell at his feet, intestines strung over their bodies by the pull of Tukker's knives as he moved on to his next opponents.

As the pincer closed, the cries and moans of battle lessened. The marines made short work of the remaining wreckers. At last only Tukker lived, surrounded by his death.

"You'll never take me, you carping bootlickers! Old Tuk'll not be taken by the likes o' you or any man!"

With quick precision, the little man slit his own throat, spurting blood over Waine and the marines closest to him.

"Leave him for the carrion eaters," Waine ordered through clenched teeth as he indicated the scattered bodies of the wreckers. "Casualty report?"

"Two dead from Swinn's squad, Captain," the boatswain reported, "three injured, one in Jaasun's squad and two in Magger's."

"Well done, men. Now let's locate the hideout and see what we've got. Johee!"

"Sir!" the boy responded. "Lassrin, let's go!"

The bloodhound started down the beach at a steady pace with the marine squads in formation behind him. In no time the sniffer ghost found the wreckers' hideaway. The marines took it over as their permanent headquarters. Waine ordered a hospital area set up and an inventory taken of the wreckers' booty, then settled to receive his reports.

"Captain?" Johee interrupted.

"Yes?"

"Captain, we don't have them all. Lassrin says there is another scent. It wasn't with the other group."

"What? How many?"

"Only two, sir. One like the others and one that is . . . different."

The bloodhound whined and lowered his ears, shaking his head from side to side.

"He's upset by the different one, sir."

"Take a full squad and find them. Our orders are explicit. No prisoners."

Lassrin led his young master and the squad to the path up the cliff. The contingent made its difficult way up the steep incline to the headland and then to the lighthouse. The ghostly bloodhound was almost bored as it trotted before the armed men. Johee and Lassrin waited outside while the marines entered the building. In short time they had returned to report only one wrecker, bound and gagged, up in the tower. They had killed him and thrown his body onto the heath.

"The other went across this moor. Guess they had a falling out," Johee said. He nodded to his ghostly hound. Lassrin once again took up the scent. The marine squad followed.

For the ectoplasmic dog, this was more exciting. The specter stretched his legs, his eerie bay echoing over the lonely headland. This was what hunting was all about, running the prey to ground and then ripping it to shreds. Lassrin couldn't have been more delighted. Phosphorescent drool fell from his green-gleaming fangs as he closed for the kill.

The hairs at the base of Arpad Zen's skull stood on end as the unearthly howl washed over him. He looked back to see four lanterns swinging in the darkness, coming in his direction.

"They've discovered my escape," he muttered

to himself as he climbed toward the ridge. "But what was that unholy call?"

As if in reply to his query, the blood-chilling howl beat at him again, sending him scrambling up the slope with a determination he hadn't thought possible.

When he reached the top, the apprentice looked back over the moor. The disembodied lights were making swift passage over the rough land—and something was leading them. He cast an observation spell. To his surprise, it worked. What Arpad Zen saw gave him reason to tremble with dread.

"A hound, but like no other in this world," he said, quavering.

Lassrin loomed in Arpad Zen's sight as a fiend, a bright red ectoplasmic hunter whose glowing eyes pierced the night like daggers aimed at his heart. The hound's nose showed a dark crimson, quivering as it caught the scent— his scent.

The apprentice bolted, making no effort to find cover. He ran hard along the ridge in the direction he had last seen Morasha.

"If only I can find her," he said to himself. "Maybe together we can defeat it."

The gap closed rapidly between the harrowing hound and Zen. Lassrin, scenting the fear of his quarry, bounded ahead of the marines and his master, his feral appetite whetted with the closeness of the kill.

Zen stumbled but recovered, climbing over boulders instead of trying to find his way around them. The ghostly baying sounded closer. The apprentice dared not look back, fearing what he would see. He stepped wrong, catching his ankle between two upthrust rocks, wrenching it painfully.

The sniffer ghost climbed the ridge now. Zen saw it clearly, its dark red glow a deadly smudge as it flashed across the land toward him. Zen jerked his ankle free, tearing flesh away, twisting the bones in their joint.

Zen ran his hardest, now in the complete grip of panic as he stumbled into a copse of giant oak. There was no time. The apprentice climbed a tree just as the devil hound burst into the copse, baying his bloodlust to the brooding sky.

Chapter Eight

✛ ✛ ✛

"BE AWAY, RUSALKA," the Lord Chelonia shouted in warning. "Do not let the evil take you. Be away! Live that you may find an answer to this terror of our people and redeem yourself." The giant turtle lord snapped his beak twice. His leathery head turned toward Durril and said, "Take its measure, master wizard!"

The old lord charged the Vodyanoi, gaining a masterful grip on its ruddy-black substance. He used what gifts Vila had given him long ago to wrestle with the abhorred being. Age, wisdom, and cunning helped Chelonia maneuver the Vodyanoi away from Rusalka and Durril. The old lord used a personal defense spell. With it, he honed the monster's wrath, frustrating its attempts at a quick kill. Heroically, Chelonia battled the terror, knowing his own life would be forfeit.

Rooted to the throne, Rusalka was unwilling—or unable—to move.

The Vodyanoi encompassed Lord Chelonia, oozing its jellylike ectoplasmic mass about him. As the horror began to absorb the old lord, Chelonia gathered his own life spirit. He released it, his death burning the Vodyanoi, temporarily halting the monster, depriving it of the strength and power of his soul.

Durril probed the hideous being with the observation spell. At one time it had been a physical, primitive form. He silently thanked Lord Chelonia for his sacrifice. Without the turtle lord's death, the true nature of the evil before him would have remained hidden.

Durril quaked at what his spell revealed. Before him floated a predator of immense size and insatiable appetite. Once a giant sea leech, it was now enormous, bloated with those it had killed. In some way Durril didn't understand, the Vodyanoi stole the essence of its victim's soul and turned it into an evil substance.

Nothing could stand between it and its prey.

The Vodyanoi made straight for the sea nymph. Barely slowed by the blow from the Lord Chelonia, it absorbed the stinging eels defending Rusalka. Clawlike tentacles reached for the sea nymph.

She fought the monster with all her strength and cunning, but it was clear to Durril that the sea nymph was no match for the Vodyanoi's hideous strength.

Faced with certain death, Rusalka did not

budge. She chanted, bringing the powers of storm and vortex to her aid. The angry, swirling water did not slow the predator.

"Rusalka," Durril shouted. He struggled in the guard squid's grip. "Free me, then sustain me!"

"Never!" the sea nymph said. "You have taken everything from me, but I rule here."

"Don't be foolish, Rusalka," Durril said. The Vodyanoi swirled like a malignant storm toward the beautiful sea nymph. "You cannot defeat it alone!"

Durril watched in horror as ghostly tentacles touched Rusalka's lush body. Like lightning, the giant phosphorescent squid released Durril and shot at the Vodyanoi. For a brief moment, the tentacled beast wrestled with its ancient nemesis. Then it blinked out, essence sucked up by the predator. The Vodyanoi took on a dark glow as a result of this new infusion of power.

"Sustain me, Rusalka!" Durril shouted again as he stepped between the sea nymph and the horror attacking her.

Durril chanted as fast as he could. He started again with the observation spell. The Vodyanoi wasn't all-powerful as he had feared. A weak spot where Chelonia had struck shone in a paler, weaker red. The wizard sought the bridge to his most powerful exorcism spell. The tingle of barely controlled magics crawled along his skin. He did not have enough power to do what was needed against the predator.

"Rusalka!" he called as he struggled to counter the unthinkable Vodyanoi.

Rusalka joined Durril's fight, admitting by her action that her life depended on alliance.

Durril drew from the Vodyanoi the power of its black-red aura. He bundled it into a tight ball of condensed might, then elongated it into a phantom spear.

"Rusalka, when I tell you, give me the force of your storm and the complete power of your vortex. Make it flow through me and into the spear."

The sea nymph nodded her willingness, all her concentration going into focusing her might.

"Now!" Durril shouted.

The wizard threw the dark spear of the Vodyanoi's corrupted aura back at the monster. Rusalka did as Durril ordered. All her powers flowed through him and into the spear, aiding its flight, sending it deep into the soul quenching horror precisely where the Lord Chelonia had struck and weakened it.

A bright flash temporarily blinded Durril as the sea bottom was rocked by a deafening howl.

Durril collapsed, leaving Rusalka to confront the soul-snatcher. She watched in amazement as her enemy hung suspended before her, momentarily paralyzed, the glow of its blood-red eyes pulsating erratically. It fluttered toward her.

Then it moved off, diminished but not defeated.

The Vodyanoi would return. The next time Rusalka might not be so lucky. Her kingdom would never be hers until this great menace was destroyed. Frightened, the sea nymph knew she did not have the power to destroy the Vodyanoi.

But Durril had the ability. If she could not rule in her kingdom one way, there was another method, very old, but successful in its own right. She sat and stared at the fallen wizard until he stirred. His eyes popped open. Only when he saw the tentacled soul-eater had gone did he relax.

"When I have garnered your knowledge, wizard, I will have no more use for you. Until then, you prove useful," Rusalka whispered as she stroked Durril's brow and his fine dark hair.

Durril looked up at Rusalka's beautiful, anxious face and thought he saw angelic beings.

"You are not harmed?" she asked, her musical voice low, wrapping him with her care.

"I am well, Rusalka," Durril said, trying to sit up.

"Good, master wizard. Then we can continue with your trial."

"What?"

"We must finish your trial, Durril. This kingdom is ruled by law, not whim." She smiled prettily at him, adding to his confusion.

"But . . ." he began.

"No arguments, Durril," Rusalka said as she took her seat on the throne. "It will take some time to reassemble the court and the jury. I will summon them. Until then, you may sit here by me and tell me of your adventures. I am sure you have much to tell."

Rusalka straightened the yellow-jeweled crown, the supreme symbol of her office. Its flash caught Durril's eye, reminding him of possibilities forgotten in the frenzy of battle. Because of his narrow escape from disaster, he found it hard to begin the tale of his life as it should have been told.

Never had he encountered a being like the

Vodyanoi. His spells had some effect against it, but the process was different, altered by the water world.

"Without the old Lord Chelonia's help, I might not have seen what I was really fighting," he thought. Silently he also admitted that without Rusalka's help, he would not have been as effective as he had been.

He forced the Vodyanoi from his mind. He tried to imagine himself beginning his raree show, peasants flocking to his stage to listen to tall tales. Smiling, Durril sat beside the sea nymph at the foot of the throne. The watery light caught her burnished hair and rested in the hollow of her pale throat. Durril told her of his adventures. She listened enraptured, her amber eyes agleam, sparkling approval of his prowess until the jury returned and the court reassembled.

After the company resettled itself, Rusalka gave Durril a last secretive smile. She stood to address her retainers.

"Lords and Ladies of the court," she began. Her voice had lost its angry quality. "I report to you with great sorrow the demise of the Lord Chelonia, my most loyal of liegemen."

Murmurs of shock and grief ran through the tired body of the court. The venerable old turtle's death was a true blow to the community, many of whom had never known life without him.

"He died in defense of me against that great evil he had come to warn us against. The wisdom of his words and the gallantry of his acts will live with us forever." She paused solemnly

to honor the dead. After a few seconds a small,
twisted smile curled her lips.

"And he was right!" continued Rusalka with
renewed fervor. "The concern of this court is
not the death of the master wizard Durril, but
the destruction of the Vodyanoi. Durril joined
with me in fighting the horror. We drove it
away, but it lurks within the realm to do us
harm again."

The wizard laughed at Rusalka's inability to
accept his power as greater than her own. The
old resentment toward him lingered, barely
held in check.

"We must conclude this trial," the sea nymph
ordered. "I ask that the jury agree with my decision." She cleared her throat before continu-
ing.

"For services rendered to this kingdom, for
your protection of my life, master wizard Durril, you will have your life, but not your liberty.
The Vodyanoi is not destroyed, only diminished.

"How says the jury?" she asked.

"The jury speaks the will of the sea nymph,"
responded the ghostly carp.

"This court has spoken." Rusalka smiled at
Durril. "Master wizard Durril, you have your
life. I now charge you—"she hurried onward
without pause, preventing him from making any
protest—"to take up the quest as our defender.
Track the Vodyanoi to its lair and destroy it!"

Stunned, Durril paused before replying. He
quickly recovered, pressing what advantage he
could gain in the moment.

"The decision of the court is fair," he said,
smiling halfheartedly at the sea nymph. The

flash of surprise crossing her face warmed him. She had not expected him to agree so easily.

"I request arms. You would not want me to go unshielded after so great a menace."

"Of course, master wizard, take what you like from among my store," Rusalka said, her brilliant smile gracing Durril's request with approval. "But first, a celebration to honor your quest. Afterward, we will speak privately," the sea nymph concluded, promise heavy in her voice.

The court disbanded once again, this time to prepare for the feasting. Durril was led to private quarters to rest.

Glad of the time alone, he considered all that had occurred. Lord Chelonia had been a remarkable being. At the last, the old turtle prevented the Vodyanoi from absorbing him by dissolving his own essence. Durril had watched it through the observation spell, taking the monster's measure. Durril considered how the heroic lord had gathered his own life force and used it against the Vodyanoi. He had blocked the monster's power, denying it the chance to absorb his soul. Durril knew how it had been done; the old lord had given him that insight at the cost of his own life.

It was not a pleasant consideration, but one Durril would keep in mind if faced with the same grim circumstances. The ability Chelonia displayed came from the sea nymph Vila. What a remarkable queen she must have been, Durril reflected. No wonder his father had loved her.

Exhausted, Durril slept. Before drifting off, he recalled the heat of Rusalka's power sustaining and coursing through him. "Stand close to the fire and get burned," he muttered as he entered a dream of yellow jewels and amber eyes.

Durril was awakened by his escort, this time four pearlescent ghosts. Forming an honor guard, they led him from his chamber to a place of prominence beside the sea nymph. An ornate chair had been retrieved from somewhere in the hoard. It sat to the right of Rusalka's throne.

"Welcome, master wizard Durril," the sea nymph said.

Glowing angelfish surrounded her. Like animated jewels they flitted about in a moving arch over the throne, lighting Rusalka with an ever-changing display of twinkling color.

She wore a garment of almost transparent midnight-blue and silver scales which revealed more of her sleek, pale body than it covered. Her red hair, held by a net of pearls, was pulled back from her face and body. Durril involuntarily caught his breath, unable to reply immediately. Finally he spoke.

"Greetings, Rusalka. You are very lovely this evening."

He had not noticed how long her dark lashes were until she lowered them at his compliment.

The grotto was transformed into a wonderland of glowing color. Groups of Rusalka's retainers danced in intricate patterns throughout, providing a constantly moving display which puzzled and fascinated the eyes. Sea horses, ridden by merman jockeys, made fiery pinwheels overhead. Glowing red ectoplasmic sharks alternated with the phosphorescent squid and pulsating blue-green puffer fish to form cascading fountains about the grotto. Pink eels entwined with green morays to weave complex serpentine forms about the delicate coral pillars.

Rusalka's retainers began singing. Their flowing music formed a quivering whole with the moving light patterns of the others. Soon Durril's senses were overwhelmed by the living tapestry of sight and sound surrounding him.

"Wine, Durril?" the sea nymph asked, offering him an elaborate gold chalice inlaid with mother-of-pearl and wrapped with huge luminous rubies.

"It is very good," she encouraged, fitting the cup into his hands, her touch suggestive as it lingered over his grasp.

He drank deeply, first of her eyes and then from the cup. The vintage was strong but good. It tasted like salted honey. The potent liquid flowed through his body, easing him.

"What do you think of our festivities?" Rusalka asked. "My people do their best to honor you with their arts."

"I have never beheld such beauty," Durril said honestly, his look fastened on the sea nymph.

"It is all yours now that you belong to our realm," Rusalka whispered.

The floor surrounding them sparkled suddenly with glowing anemones, purple and white, orange, green, and mauve. Scattered among them were pulsating manta rays, their vibrating bodies evoking a spectrum of colors in syncopation with the twinkling sea flowers.

A troop of leaping porpoises tumbled before the throne, each ridden by shining silver starfish. The watery world enabled the performers to perform gymnastics no one on land dared try. Durril was taken aback by their speed and agility as they romped first in precision formations and then with comic disorganization. He laughed with true merriment at their clowning, applauding wildly at their finale.

"Bravo!" Durril cheered.

Rusalka finished her cup, then stood.

"Thank you, my people, for such a wonderful celebration. The hour is late and our day has been long. I bid you good night."

The lighted undersea world dimmed as its denizens went to their homes, leaving Rusalka and Durril alone. His ghostly escort returned to guard duty among the treasure hoard. The sea nymph dismissed the sparkling angelfish to their rest with a wave of her pale white hand. Quiet descended on the deep darkness of the grotto.

"Come with me, Durril," she whispered, her words carrying the lure and promise of ancient sirens. "We have much to discuss before you begin your perilous quest on the morrow."

Rusalka took his hand, her touch surprisingly warm and inviting. The sea nymph led him through the coral pillars to her private chamber where more of the salty-sweet wine awaited them.

The room glowed with the soft rose light of minute organisms arranging themselves in slow-moving patterns on the cavern walls. The only furniture was a great chest of gems where the sea nymph's yellow-jeweled crown rested and a soft bed that was laid in the discarded multihued shell of a giant clam.

Rusalka held out her arms to him. He went to her and they sank down into the cushioned clamshell.

Chapter Nine

❖ ❖ ❖

ARPAD ZEN CLUNG terrified to the central trunk of the oak as the ghostly sniffer hound scrabbled below, bellowing his frustration to the troops following. Zen saw the bobbing lights begin their ascent of the ridge.

Frantic, the apprentice started the transmutation spell in an attempt to silence the loudly baying hound. Halfway through, he stopped the chant, having no clear idea of what he would transmute the specter into.

Cheers from the hound's owners assaulted his ears.

Desperation seized him. Zen chanted, linking the transmutation spell with what he could remember of an exorcism spell Durril had used in the Valley of the Ultimate Demise. At first, he thought nothing was happening. Slowly the tingle and shift of a working spell surrounded him. He chanted faster, closing his eyes, concentrating all his energy and hope in the spell.

Below him the angry baying was cut short by a surprised yelp of intense pain.

Zen opened his eyes, daring to look at his vicious attacker. He kept chanting, his hands

shaking, making unreliable the grip he had on
the tree.

Something had happened. The ferocious ghost
hound wavered, whining, and retreated from
the base of the tree. It turned, tail between its
insubstantial legs, to stumble, then fall, its
bloodred color turning paler as it attempted to
crawl away.

Zen did not wait. He shimmied down the tree
and ran as fast as he could from the copse.
Without slowing, he hurtled down the ridge on
the side opposite the sea. Just over the top, he
lost his footing and rolled to the bottom. Even
if the spectral dog was hampered by his spell,
its owners were not. They were close behind.

"That unholy hound doesn't belong to the
wreckers, of that I'm sure," he reasoned to himself as he strove to bisect the rough heath,
heading for a larger woods. "Who does own it?"
Zen wondered fearfully, limping onward.

Johee and the squad breached the copse minutes after Arpad Zen's departure. They split up,
looking for Lassrin and their fugitive. The small
group of trees greeted them with a foreboding
silence after the bold calls from their ghostly
hunting dog.

"Lassrin. Lassrin!" Johee cried, suddenly
afraid. "Lassrin, where are you? Lassrin, come
here!"

The boy stood mute, listening for his partner's familiar woof. It didn't come. What did
reach his ears was a mournful whine and the
soft, slow rustle of leaves.

"Lassrin, where are you?" Johee called in
alarm.

He almost stumbled over the sniffer hound as

it crawled toward him, its bloody countenance now a pale, sickly pink.

"Lassrin! No, Lassrin!"

Johee knelt beside the diminishing ghost hound, gathering the specter's frail ectoplasmic flesh into his arms.

"No Lassrin, you can't . . . you can't dissolve!" the boy cajoled.

With a final moan and a weak wagging of its tail, the sniffer ghost vanished, leaving only the cruel night air and darkness for its master to hold.

"No!" Johee shouted to the winds. "No!" he wailed, his hands grasping only one another as tears poured from his eyes.

"Come, lad," a hardened marine said as he grabbed him. "Pull yourself together. We'll hunt no more tonight."

Arpad Zen crawled the final few feet into cover in the small forest. His injured ankle had finally given way and refused to support him. That, along with his need for food and the general harrowing of the flight, left him drained. He struggled to find a hideout, not knowing that his pursuers had given up the chase. A stand of bracken gave some shelter. From it he saw the outline of the ridge and the copse from which he had escaped as a darker stain against the night sky. Before he could stop himself, Zen fell asleep in his prickly accommodations.

Close after midnight the apprentice awakened, all senses alerted to danger. He probed the dark immediately surrounding him. Then he heard it; an angry sound of shouting came from the direction of the ridge. The copse where he had been burst into flame, brightening the night sky with incandescent orange light.

Something ran from the wood and the fire, chased by men carrying torches. For only a moment, Zen saw the victim of the chase, but the glimpse was enough.

"Morasha!" Zen croaked. "Morasha . . ."

One clear call came to the apprentice, carried on a gust of wind from the sea.

"Kill the ogre!"

The pursuit disappeared over the ridge.

Quickly, Arpad Zen crawled from his protecting cover to reverse his path. He hobbled toward the damnable ridge as fast as his injury would allow. Even as the slowness of his pace frustrated him, it also goaded him on.

Morasha had vanished over the ridge, traveling away from the lighthouse. For that the apprentice was grateful. He never wanted to see the lighthouse with its accursed burning ghost or the treacherous wreckers again.

As he topped the rise, he spotted torches some distance along it, moving inland.

"At least they haven't caught her yet," he consoled himself as he lurched onward on his game foot. "She will blame me if they do, I know it!"

But Zen did not go very far. From out of the night came hundreds of glowing green specters. They marched toward him, locking him within their ghostly ring.

Released by the death of the wrecking crew, the ghosts of the dead merchant crewmen now claimed revenge—on him!

"Stop, knave, dastard who steals life from honest men! Now that we have found you, you shall not escape our judgment!"

Zen froze in his steps. His breath came in short, shallow gasps.

"But . . ."

"Silence!" roared a distinguished ship's captain leading the ghostly crew. "You will have your chance to speak soon enough. But not now. Come!"

The captain headed back down the ridge to the moor below and then toward the sea. Arpad Zen was herded by a contingent of armed apparitions, their ectoplasmic daggers edged with shining silver malice.

The apprentice started to cast a spell, but the words died in his throat. What had happened with the sniffer hound had been luck, a freak chance in the awkward combination of his spells. However, Zen was not a master wizard. He lacked the skills required to defeat this company of dead souls. They would do with him what they liked. He followed them unwillingly across the moor.

Zen looked back once. The minute torches still shone, moving away from him.

"At least Morasha is still free." He hoped the ogre familiar would get away and rescue him.

"But how can she," he silently chided himself, "when she doesn't even know where I am? And why would she want to? I've brought her nothing but misery."

In quick lockstep, the escort marched Zen to the cliff edge. He thought they intended to march him over the edge to his death on the jagged rocks below. But the captain halted the company just short of walking into space.

"You will remain here," he said to Arpad Zen,

"under guard. Not all have assembled yet. We will not begin until every one of us is present."

Before he could respond, the captain and most of his retinue vanished. Zen was left surrounded by a small group of angry specters who stood shoulder to shoulder around him, creating an effective barrier against his escape. All the apprentice could do was sit on the cold rock and wait.

Near dawn the ghostly captain returned, his company increased to almost double its previous size. Hundreds of ghosts of long-dead crewmen hung over the moor and floated in the brisk sea winds gusting over the cliff.

"Stand up," the captain commanded Zen. "Stand and be judged."

Arpad Zen jumped, galvanized by the order. The circle around him widened as the phantoms assembled themselves into a court.

"I am Captain Korrgan, late of the merchanter *Venture*. I will act as your prosecutor and judge of this court. Your jury is made of up the captains and first mates from the scores of ships run aground on this foul shore."

Without stopping, the wrathful ghost hurried on, anxious to finish the proceedings.

"You are charged with the purposeful wrecking of ships and the deaths of their honorable and innocent crews. How do you plead?" Korrgan demanded.

"Not . . ." The apprentice swallowed. He fought to gain his composure. He was used to exorcising ghosts, not being judged by them. "Not guilty!" Zen stated as convincingly as possible.

The members of the jury shook their heads in

negation, but their response was cut short by the prosecuting captain.

"Duly noted," Korrgan said.

Zen studied the jury for the first time. All its members glared at him from unflinching eyes aglow with a thirst for vengeance. He gulped, then nervously coughed.

"We will continue," his interrogator said, interrupting Zen's observations.

"Are you not part of the wrecking gang?" the captain asked.

"No," Zen said, his voice stronger this time. "I am not a member of that unholy gang."

"But you served its purposes," the captain accused.

"No, I did not," Zen retorted.

"The evidence of your crime faces you. All here died because of the wreckers and their wickedness. How can you not admit that you served them? We are here now because they have met their deserved end. *You* are the last!"

"What do you mean, met their end?" Zen questioned in return.

"Fellow seafarers have put an end to their horrible work. This very night their bodies lie on the beach, left for scavengers. This is justice for what they scavenged. You are the only one left, and we will have our justice from you! Did you not aid the wreckers by tampering with the light?"

"No . . . yes, but not as you think," the apprentice stammered in confusion.

"Did you tamper with the light, causing the beacon to be inconstant, luring us to our deaths?" the relentless captain pressed.

"I cannot deny it," Arpad Zen said. "But it was not as you think."

"You will have your time to speak, you foul murderer. For now, be still."

Captain Korrgan approached the jury. He stood with vaporous arms crossed on his chest, legs spread wide and head tilted to one side. He looked at the bedraggled apprentice in silent menace.

After a time long enough to make Zen fidget, the ghost captain said, "I submit to you, members of this jury, that the one before you was instrumental in our coming to harm. You have heard him admit his guilt. He who tampered with the beacon so necessary to the safe passage along these shores. Our only decision is the mode of his death—there can be no other conclusion. Our spirits will never rest until we have our accounting.

"His death will not save us from the tormented wandering through eternity to which we have been doomed. We cannot rest. We will have only our satisfaction at having achieved revenge to console us! It will be enough!"

Captain Korrgan retired to one side of the ghostly circle, his prosecution finished.

Only the whistling of the predawn wind sounded on the headland. Arpad Zen shivered in the chill of its passage. He would not quail before these accusing specters. Durril's voice echoed in his head: "Better a sword in the front . . . better a sword in the front . . ."

"Do you have a name?" an unexpectedly gentle voice asked.

Zen looked toward the jury. One ghost nodded encouragement, prompting him to answer.

"Yes, yes, I have a name. I am Arpad Zen, apprentice to the master wizard Durril," he said.

"Then we will have your story, Arpad Zen. Ours you know already. Speak and we will listen."

The apprentice did not know where to begin. The cold and his injured ankle tugged at him. He was hungry, and there was still Morasha's fate to worry about.

"I've never been a good storyteller," Zen began. "No one lets me finish any tale I start."

The apprentice stopped and got hold of himself.

"My master, the wizard Durril and I, and Morasha, our familiar who is in ogre form . . . we, we were passengers on the *Pitcairn* bound for Wonne. My master knew all along something was wrong. He said as much, but even he could not figure it out."

"Apprentice Zen," another juror interrupted. "How came you to this shore? That is of interest to us, not your master's quandary."

"Yes, of course," Arpad replied, licking his dry lips. "The *Pitcairn* went down in a vortex. That is, it didn't go down. My master prevented its being sucked into the vortex which was a conjuration, but the ship broke apart between the spell and counterspell. There had been a mutiny, and we created a vision of a sea serpent to try to stop it. Because my master used his ability, we were detected, I am sure of it. And Morasha was seasick all along, but Durril couldn't cure it."

"Arpad Zen, how came you to this shore and

your interference with the light?" an angry spectral voice demanded.

"That's what I'm getting at," the apprentice said in exasperation.

"Let him tell the tale as he must," Captain Korrgan ordered. "It is the only way we will have the whole of it." Korrgan gestured and demanded, "Proceed."

"Yes, thank you," Zen replied miserably, thinking to himself, "I try even the patience of ghosts." Gamely, he continued.

"The ship, the *Pitcairn*, went down. That is, it broke apart in the battle of the spells. At first Durril and I were together, but he had to save his kit, and Morasha couldn't swim well and needed help. So I went to help her. But a real storm had come up and we were separated from Durril.

"Morasha and I were in the sea a long time. It was not good for her and she will never let me forget it, I know. From somewhere I got a piece of the mizzenmast, and Morasha chased away the sharks because the water caused her to stink dreadfully.

"Then we saw the light and the sea pushed us toward it. The mizzenmast broke on the reef. Morasha was swept onto the other side. I thought I'd killed her again and there was nothing to bind her to. But I know she is alive now because I've seen her."

"And how did you tamper with the light, man?" a ghostly spectator asked with considerable impatience.

"I was washed farther down the shore and must have been thrown over the reef, I don't know how. I was knocked out and awoke surrounded by Tukker and his gang. They found out that I am a wizard's apprentice and decided not to kill me. They made me entertain them, but I'm not good at tricks, and they didn't like my jokes—"

"The light, man!" A chorus of voices echoed around the circle.

"Tukker locked me in the lighthouse. He said that if I didn't exorcise the ghost of the damned man which burned as a beacon, he would kill me," Zen blurted out.

"A burning ghost?" Captain Korrgan demanded, taken aback.

"Yes, a damned man, cursed to burn eternally as beacon on this coast in a fire that would not consume him. But I couldn't do it," Zen finished in a rush.

"You would not relieve the tortured soul?" Korrgan roared in anger.

"No, no," the apprentice pleaded. "I could not. I do not have the skill. I have never exorcised anything, except a few minor poltergeists and something"—he paused—"something which chased me. I didn't know I could do it but I was in the tree and—"

"What happened to the burning ghost?" his prosecutor demanded, cutting off another of Zen's ramblings.

"I transmuted him."

"What?"

"I transmuted him. I tried all the other spells I remembered and none worked. Tukker was going to kill me if the ghost still burned. So I tried the transmutation spell Durril uses when he does his raree show. I didn't think it was working until the room filled with mist. It didn't stay long, but he was very grateful for the relief. Tukker made me transmute him again because he blinked, and that confused the ships and the wreckers were happy."

The jury murmured among itself. Zen caught phrases, but nothing they said sounded very encouraging.

"Did you know the results of your work, apprentice?" Captain Korrgan asked, calling the court back to order.

"Yes," Arpad sadly admitted. "I had no choice. If I did not transmute the burning ghost, the wreckers would take my life. Because I interfered with him, I have cost you yours," Zen said dejectedly.

"I meant no harm. I do not have the power of full exorcism," Zen said. "My master, Durril, has tried to teach me well, but I lack initiative, he always says. Only the burning specter achieved some relief."

"At what cost, Arpad Zen?" Captain Korrgan asked harshly.

Shouts wafted aloft from the beach below, interrupting the deliberations of the spectral court.

The rhythmical chant beat at Arpad Zen. He rushed to the cliff's edge and looked over.

"Kill the ogre! Kill the ogre! Kill the ogre!" rang on the dawn air.

"Morasha!" the young apprentice cried. "Run, Morasha! Save yourself!"

But Arpad Zen's words were thrown back into his face by the strong sea breeze.

Morasha stumbled along the beach, hostile villagers close behind her. Zen saw that she was almost exhausted. Even worse, she was unaware that her direction would take her to the merchant marine headquarters.

"What is being hunted so fiercely, apprentice?" Captain Korrgan demanded. "You act as if you know."

"It is Morasha, my master's familiar. She is in ogre form now. If the villagers catch her and kill her, she will dissolve because there is no one to do a binding spell for her to attain a new body.

"She will blame me for killing her again. This time she will be right," Zen said disconsolately.

"Can you do such a spell, apprentice?"

"I don't know. I know how it is done, but I've never done it unassisted by my master," Zen said, wringing his hands as Morasha turned a corner and was lost from sight, the angry chase following close behind her.

The first rays of dawn sunlight painted the headland a garish red. Zen was reminded of blood—his blood.

"We must conclude this trial," the captain abruptly announced. "It is dawn and the time of our eternal pain is upon us once more."

Zen watched as the morning light touched the ghostly beings' ectoplasmic substance. Blue lines like tiny lightning bolts danced over the surfaces of the apparitions' bodies, visible marks of their inward suffering. Zen had been told that ghosts of innocent murder victims suffered greatly during the day because they pined for life still. Bright sunlight starkly displayed life's richness that was no longer theirs.

"Have you anything further to say in your defense, apprentice Arpad Zen?" Captain Korrgan asked, his voice betraying the pain he suffered.

"Nothing, Captain. If my master were here, he could relieve you, and maybe Morasha, too. But I am inept," Arpad Zen apologized. "What I did was in defense of my own life. I do not know if you can understand that since I have cost you yours."

"The jury will now retire to deliberate and pass judgment on you," the captain said.

Once again the apprentice was encircled by a small contingent of ghosts. He watched the sun rise higher in the blue sky. The angry cries from below had ceased. Arpad Zen did not know Morasha's fate but was sure of his own as he gazed forlornly on the desolate headland and the rocky coast of Pellas' kingdom.

How could the ghostly court return any verdict but guilty?

Chapter Ten
✛ ✛ ✛

"THAT ONE," DURRIL said, pointing to an unimposing iron sword covered with corrosion. Only the hilt shone brightly because of an intricate wrapping of gold and silver wire. The pommel was a jet-black stone.

"I have others which are more befitting a defender of the realm," Rusalka protested, surprised at his choice. "This one belonged to a king." The sea nymph pointed to a gold-covered bronze sword whose hilt glittered with inlaid

rubies and sapphires. Emerald-eyed twin drag-
ons formed the pommel of the princely weapon.

"No." Durril refused with polite firmness.
"This one will do quite well." He hefted the battered old weapon appreciatively. It fit his hand
as if it had been made for him, balancing perfectly just in front of the hilt.

"This is not a proper weapon," the sea nymph
said, shaking her head at the inexplicable ways
of men, "but do what you like. You must have
a proper sheath, though."

She took the tooled green leather scabbard
and belt from the king's sword and strapped it
about Durril's waist. Her fingers lingered as she
touched him, then her eyes rose to catch his.
She smiled in remembered delight.

"Are you ready?"

"Yes, Rusalka. Farewell for now." Durril bent
forward, briefly touching the sea nymph's inviting lips with his own. Pulling away reluctantly,
he turned to the waiting squid.

"Are you sure you want to accompany me,
Boorgan?"

"Yes, master wizard Durril," the phosphorescent being replied without hesitation. "I am the
only one who can help you now. It is my duty,
and my privilege. The Lord Chelonia was right.
This evil must be destroyed before it destroys
us all."

"Let's not tarry. The Vodyanoi is waiting for
us," Durril said, accepting his new partner's al-
legiance.

Durril and Boorgan disappeared into the
darkness of the undersea world. Durril found
the going easier than before. This time the mas-

ter wizard was cradled within the beast's glowing tentacles rather than imprisoned there.

Rusalka waved to Durril until he was out of sight. He watched and wondered at her. She had wished him a speedy return, hinting at unfinished business with him. If it was more business like the night before, Durril knew he would find the time for her. Suspicions of a darker purpose in her caresses troubled him, though.

Boorgan swam long hours, going deeper and deeper into the sea. Durril grew restive as the light dimmed because of their extreme depth; only that small glow produced by the phosphorescent creature lit a small bubble around them. It was as if Durril traveled into the void to be swallowed and never seen again.

Their passage was silent. Durril knew they made progress only by the pressure of water moving past him and the shining creature vibrating as he propelled them rapidly along. After an eternity of darkness, Boorgan slowed and then stopped.

"Have we arrived?" Durril asked.

"I think so," Boorgan said. "I am the only one in the sea nymph's realm with knowledge of the Vodyanoi's lodging. And what I know is not firsthand but passed to me through the generations. My information may be only stories to frighten children into behaving but I believe it to be true. My people do not like intimidation."

"Where are we?" the wizard asked.

"This is the Forbidden Defile. It is said that the Vodyanoi lives nearby. I have never been here before, nor do I know anyone who has. This location is part of our lore," Boorgan explained.

"Then we must search, my trusty friend. How big is this Forbidden Defile?"

"I am sorry, master wizard. I know so little. It is vast, but there are no tales of even the most adventurous returning from the Defile," the squid said.

Uneasily Durril dismounted to stand on the rough sea floor. The broken rock underfoot gave him difficult purchase as he started to explore. Boorgan burned as brightly as he could to provide light for Durril's reconnaissance. The best he could determine, the scarred and broken rock extended to Pellas' island. From small spoor left on the jagged rock, it was clear they did indeed trespass on the Vodyanoi's domain. The magical residue made Durril dizzy with its power.

And this was only a fraction of the Vodyanoi's might!

Durril finally remounted and let Boorgan cross the extensive barrier. They reached the end of the broken land only to drop even farther down into the depths.

Durril trusted his passage to Boorgan and worked carefully, casting the observation spell. He shielded the working magic, not wanting to alert the Vodyanoi.

The more he reviewed what Lord Chelonia helped to reveal about the predator, the more Durril was convinced that it was the magical instrument of an old master wizard from the Spell Wars. Rahman'dur had survived, protected by the Valley of the Ultimate Demise on Loke-Bor. It was not unreasonable that a second survivor from those disastrous wars hid here, secure under the Mother Ocean's watery

skirts. It was the only explanation for the Vodyanoi's hideous power. Durril renewed his efforts to shield his observation spell, working
slowly and carefully as Boorgan traveled downward into what had to be a bottomless pit.

What Durril saw confused him—he saw
nothing. It was total, absolute *nothingness*. He
detected no forms, living or ectoplasmic, in the
surrounding water. He saw no landscape. Even
the water lay beyond his ability to espy. His
vision penetrated only darkness and more darkness. Whatever Durril had entered, it revealed
naught to his sight, whether magical or normal.

Uneasily, the wizard's hand sought the sword
he had so impulsively chosen. Surprised, he felt
heat radiating from the black stone in the pommel. He cupped his hand over the stone. The
tingle of magic ran through his hand and arm.

"I was right!" he said to himself.

Durril had chosen the shabby weapon precisely because it was the only one in Rusalka's
huge store which was not eye-catching. Long
ago his father told him of an ancient sword of
power which lay unclaimed in the Mother
Ocean because it was shabby and common-
place. Durril had hoped he had found it when
he spotted the ordinary iron of the weapon, and
now he rejoiced.

He drew the sword, holding it before him,
blade downward. Once again Durril cast the
carefully shielded observation spell, but this
time he focused it through the warm black
stone of the pommel.

"Boorgan! Stop!" Durril ordered.

The wizard's vision cleared suddenly. Durril

had halted Boorgan within the confines of an inverted cone in the sandy ocean floor.

"Do not move swiftly, Boorgan. We are too close," the wizard said to his partner.

Boorgan hung suspended and motionless, obeying Durril's command.

"We are almost in the Vodyanoi's trap. Can you turn and start upward?"

"I can try, Durril," Boorgan answered quietly. "I see nothing."

"We are in a huge cone-shaped sand pit. Something waits at the bottom, not far from us. Strong movement will alert it to our presence. It glows ravenous and malevolent in my magical sight," Durril explained. He turned slowly, studying the sandy bottom and finding more residue than before. The power locked in this magical detritus almost blinded him.

"This is the entrance to the Vodyanoi's lair," he said softly. "I see traces of its passage—recent spoor. If you can get us out of here, maybe we can figure a way around the monster thing guarding this portal."

"I will try, Durril," Boorgan said.

Slowly, Boorgan tightened his hold on Durril. Equally slowly he reversed his position so that his head faced upward out of the sand entrapment. Durril now hovered over the horrid ambusher hidden in the bottom of the well.

"When I give the order, Boorgan, move as fast as you can," the wizard said.

"I understand, Durril."

Bringing the black stone to eye level, Durril surveyed the floor of the sand pit closely. No doubt remained. The Vodyanoi had passed through here. Slight traces of the broken aura were scattered like deadly snowflakes on the sandy bottom. Beneath them lurked an orange and crimson beast composed mostly of mouths filled with butchering magenta fangs.

"Now!" Durril commanded.

Boorgan responded immediately, shooting upward. Too late! The cunning sea ant collapsed his trap, sucking the wizard and Boorgan toward its waiting jaws.

"Hold tight," Durril shouted. He had maintained the observation spell as a matter of habit. Now he struck with a swift spell of exorcism as the sea ant's mouths fastened about them.

In a flurry of orange dust, the voracious beast dissolved, leaving the wizard and his companion trapped beneath the collapsed sand cone in the anteroom of the Vodyanoi's lair.

"Quick, Boorgan, this way!"

They moved to the left only to be confronted with another twist and turn, finding themselves back in the anteroom.

"It's a maze," Durril said, confounded, "and cunningly laid. It defies my spell, Boorgan. Let's look at this again."

Durril decided that he could no longer employ the cloaking spell he used to hide his observations. By some counterspell he did not understand, his cunning worked against him.

"Very clever of that old wizard," he thought, "very resourceful, indeed."

Durril faced a wizard of tremendous power.

"Whoever approaches, especially if they are adept, will be detected."

Without hesitation, Durril lifted his sword

and chanted, focusing again through the black stone. The illusions surrounding him cleared. Or were these even more slyly contrived illusions?

"To our left, Boorgan, and to our left again. That wall is a conjuration. We will pass through it into the main passage of this craftily laid puzzle."

The giant squid did as directed, moving cautiously. Boorgan paused only an instant in front of the seemingly solid wall, then continued, swimming through easily into the first chamber of the Vodyanoi's well-protected lair.

Boorgan was immediately blinded by light reflected from the crystal mirror walls of the chamber arching over them. He dimmed his phosphorescence but still the light assaulted him, hurting his large, sensitive eyes. He had no defense against the omnidirectional radiant attack.

Rapidly Durril surveyed the room, attempting to scout a path. He, too, was almost blinded by the reflected brilliance of the light. Squinting, he thought the radiance intensified as it bounced off the fractured facets of the walls.

"Release your ink," Durril ordered.

Boorgan did as ordered. The smoky dark bile permeated the room. It clung to the crystal surfaces, allowing both Durril and the squid to find their way out of the confusing chamber of light and mirrors.

The escape passage was narrow and lay between two jagged-edged slabs projecting from the wall. Durril shot an exorcism spell through it, knowing they would have no room to maneuver once they entered the confining hall.

Violet and green explosions burst throughout the narrow passageway as ectoplasmic sea scorpions dissolved against the walls and high, vaulted ceiling.

"All clear now. Let's get out of here," Durril said.

Boorgan moved forward through the unpleasant gate into a stunning grotto with a smooth floor of silver sand. The wizard sucked in his breath; a tiny column of bubbles rose from his lips. The silver floor was yet another canny illusion. It disguised a spiral ramp which reached again downward. What awaited beyond the ramp Durril did not want to contemplate.

Writhing over one another, thousands of venomous snakes waited for the unwary. Their mottled skin showed lavender, scarlet, and rusty red. As they opened their mouths, yellow fangs dripped corrosive juices. The dreadful snakes paralleled the narrow spiral ramp, making a tightly packed and deadly wall around it.

"You cannot come farther, Boorgan. No, wait." Durril cut short his companion's protest.

He described the scene from hell to Boorgan. "You cannot negotiate the way. It will be certain death for you. Wait for me here. I'll ward you as best I can before I go. There are too many serpents for me to destroy outright, but it looks as if the path provides safe passage through them." He did not add that walking it would be the act of a suicidal fool.

Hefting his sword, Durril stepped onto the spiral way and ran. He negotiated it without challenge, which surprised him. The monstrous snakes took no notice of his passage. Quickly

Durril reached the bottom of the ramp to find he had blundered into a nest of sharks.

"They are physical," he noted, astounded. Everything he had encountered until now had been a ghostly remnant or potent conjuration set upon him by an unseen wizard.

He slashed the underbelly of a shining white monster coming for him. Just in time, he turned to meet the challenge of its mate. Durril set his sword, allowing the creature to ram into it. The iron sword with its deceptively dull blade cut cleanly through the body.

The wizard found himself the center of a frenzy as he hacked and slashed in the bloody water, barely defending himself. Durril chanted but stopped, remembering to first bring the observation spell into play. He had almost paralyzed himself—loss of mobility now would have been disastrous.

Focusing through the black stone, Durril caught the magical image of the trap he'd fallen into. The sharks were physical, but they had been mutated. What blood ran in their veins was a virulent red tide—and he had covered himself with the swift-acting poison.

The only thing protecting him was his personal defense spell. Durril felt it slipping away.

Desperately, the wizard sought an escape. He could see nothing through the red haze surrounding him. Durril searched for the deadly agent itself. He found it lying hot within each minute cell surrounding him.

Chanting a fire spell, he spread the magical flame through the poisoned water until every drop of the deadly stuff encasing him sizzled and exploded. Durril worked against time as he battled the never-tiring sharks. Swiftly the wizard followed with a freezing spell, radiating away so that he would not be consumed by his own conflagration.

It worked. Durril stood in the center of the horrible chamber as fine, gray ash settled to the floor, covering the bodies of the dead sharks.

Barely stopping for breath, he plowed through the illusory coral web forming the doorway to the next compartment—but not so fast as to enter unawares.

Before him stretched a forest of gently waving fronds, glistening iridescent colors bewitching the eye. They hung from high above him, thin and graceful in their movements. When they touched one another, the forest resounded with a melody like tinkling bells.

"Beautiful," Durril said almost reverently, "except for their killing touch."

The fronds oozed a stinging excretion, each razor-sharp edge outlined with an ultraviolet maliciousness. Swimming among them was a twisted, hideously scarred creature, a symbiotic partner existing on the pain inflicted by the death-dealing tentacles. The flesh of the tortured beast was so badly damaged that it looked like an intentional parody—but Durril was certain it had once been a man.

Durril faced an enormous man-of-war, changed by a wizard's perverted skill into this inverted forest of destruction. Inhabiting the unexpected forest was the enigma before him.

Durril cast a summoning spell on the swimming creature, calling it to him as a guide. The unsightly being fought, but Durril overcame the resistance. The wizard's stomach turned when he realized that the scarred remnant fought to increase its pleasure from the pain inflicted by contesting the spell's magical pull. Although it fought, it soon floated obediently before him.

"Take me through the forest of fronds, whatever you are," Durril ordered.

"Once man and wizard like you," the grotesquerie croaked, startling Durril. A note of old authority rang in its voice.

"Man?" Durril sneered in contempt.

"Yes, man and wizard, like you." It rasped at him, opaque eyes sunken behind angry purple scars. "But the powers here are too strong for any man to control, and soon," it slobbered, "soon they have you in their thrall!"

"Who are you?" Durril demanded, offended by the loathsome creature.

"I am Hohrman'dur, last of the great wizards." It cackled insanely. "I bid you welcome to my home. I built it myself," the repulsive beast said, its words spilling over with possessive pride.

The twisted being brushed against the fronds, a look of deep happiness crossing its misshapen face as a new poison-filled, bleeding cut appeared in its corrupted hide. It closed over, almost immediately, festering and turning a putrescent green.

Durril sickened but did not release control over the odious thing in front of him.

"You will take me through the frond forest, Hohrman'dur. You will guide me safely from this chamber of death to the passage out of it," the wizard ordered.

"And if I don't?" Hohrman'dur challenged.

"Then . . ." Durril paused to think. What torture could he visit upon this wretch? A slow smile crossed the master wizard's lips as an idea occurred to him. "I shall stop hurting you," Durril answered.

"Follow," Hohrman'dur whined in submission.

Durril entered the forest of deadly fronds. He dared to grip the scarred neck of the loathsome beast guiding him. Slowly, Hohrman'dur wove through the living strings of death. Durril saw a rhythm to the fronds' movements which his monstrous guide understood. This time, instead of lashing himself with the stinging tentacles, Hohrman'dur made his way around them, content with the lash of Durril's spell.

He stopped in front of an enormous archway. "We are here, master," he crooned. "As my reward, will you . . . hurt me?"

The wizard tried to ignore the perverted request. Durril noted the smudges of black-red ectoplasm against the pillar supporting the arch. He had come at last to the Vodyanoi's lair.

"Hohrman'dur," Durril said, gratefully releasing his grip on the grotesquerie, "why did you do it?"

"Do what, master wizard?" The mass of scar tissue laughed in mockery. "Do what?"

"Why did you fight the Spell Wars? Why did you make the Vodyanoi?" Durril surprised himself. He felt no animosity toward this creature—only pity flowed from his heart. But he needed to know what had caused the older wizards to become consumed by such insanity.

The beast ignored him, rubbing against a sharp rock that ripped his flesh from his bones.

The sight of such self-inflicted injury sparked Durril's wrath.

"Answer me!" Durril cried, fixing his command with the force of a truth spell, drilling it into the horrible flesh of the once-man before him.

"Ah . . ." Hohrman'dur quaked with joy. "Ah . . . wizard," he said, sobbing in delight. "For pleasure!" Hohrman'dur jeered. "It pleasured me, master wizard!"

Durril lashed out with his sword of power, striking a blow which should have cleaved the monstrosity in two. The weapon only ignited tendrils of raw, red flame that seared Hohrman'dur's body, sending him once again into ecstasy.

Giving pleasure was not the wizard's intent. He needed a different approach. Durril focused through the black stone, calling forth the nature of the sword. It had been forged of iron from the core of the world, beaten and shaped by an ancient son of the Mother Ocean. All it needed was a honing spell to release its power.

Durril called into play just such a spell, learned in the Valley of the Ultimate Demise. He sent it creeping along the edge of the blade. The sword sprang to magical life in Durril's hands, singing its song of desire, crying out its thirst for gore.

Hohrman'dur stood entranced before Durril's blade. The wizard swung with all his might. This time he cut through Hohrman'dur, forever ending his life.

Thrown back against the hard pillar at the entrance to the Vodyanoi's lair, Durril fell to his knees as he clung to the strength of the now quiet sword.

"Now only you remain." Durril addressed the Vodyanoi hiding somewhere in its cavern. He stood, passed the sword through the water to clean its edge and entered the vast doorway, not seeing the warning carved above it.

"If You Would Pass This Way, Abandon All Hope."

Far to the rear of the cave, Durril sighted the malevolent black-red glow of the predator. The only other light in the chamber came from his sword's shining edge. Blackness cloaked all else. Nothing showed in his observation spell, but this had been expected. He faced tremendous magical power.

Durril advanced toward the soul snatcher.

Immediately he was enmeshed by wire-thin tentacles, their stinging poisons paralyzing him. Durril lashed out with the sword, cutting an arc. As the blade passed through the invisible trap, sickly yellow-green sparks burst about him, falling to the floor where they lay pulsating wrathfully.

The wizard carefully laid the blade against his legs, using its iron edge to free himself from the vicious net.

"Where?" he gasped, focusing the observation spell through the black stone once more.

There was nothing. And then he saw . . . it.

Miraculously, the Vodyanoi had not spied him. The creature rested on a gigantic pile of bones, busy in the slow process of absorbing their calcified essence.

Durril did not tarry. Cutting a path through the invisible entrapment of wirelike ectoplasm, muttering spells to dissolve it, the wizard charged toward the predator.

The ancient sword sang its bloodlust and desire, filling the cavern with the echoes of its purpose. Any army in the Plenn Archipelagoes would have turned and run had it faced such a weapon. The Vodyanoi finally noticed Durril.

It attacked.

Durril feinted and tried to end its foul existence with a single thrust. He failed. It wrapped itself about the sword, clinging tenaciously as Durril tried to slash and hack. The creature sucked the sword's power into itself, its black-red glow heating until the monster was a burning coal. Durril fought—in vain. No matter how he turned, where he thrust, he failed to destroy the Vodyanoi.

Durril's worst fear came to pass. The sword shattered, leaving only the hilt with a jagged remnant of the blade.

The wizard staggered backward, losing his footing among the gnawed and sucked bones. He caught at anything he touched to stop the monster, throwing what he could at the advancing predator. He battered it with a leg bone, then peppered it with smaller fragments of what once had been men.

Durril grabbed a skull and flung it at the Vodyanoi's burning eyes, then another and another. His hand closed about another skull. Durril stopped when he realized what he had found.

"Kill sailors, will you!" he ranted. "Eat sea nymphs, will you!" He shouted new taunts at the great evil sweeping down upon him. And he feared nothing.

The wizard had found his own master's skull.

Once again he had access to wisdom beyond his own.

Durril held both sword hilt and skull close as he was suffocated by the oozing slime of the evil horror. It flooded over him, covering and stifling him. Durril chanted, calling through the black stone for the true nature of the beast which now devoured him.

Never had he encountered a being of such gruesome nature. The Vodyanoi was a composite of all the souls it had taken. Their essence, their power, distilled into pure evil. Its mightiest components were those who had been most good. The monster predator had twisted their goodness, perverted it to its own horrible ends. It had grown in power and ability and had become unstoppable.

Invading the innermost parts of Durril's soul, the Vodyanoi loosened Durril's identity, pulling at it, sucking it into its own horrible, bloated substance. Durril fought hard against the shift, but he had no defense against the consuming power of the giant leacher of souls.

"Never!" Durril managed to call in defiance between his gritted teeth, clutching his master's skull to his breast, an ineffective amulet. Unable to do anything else against the devouring Vodyanoi, he began the process the Lord Chelonia had so bravely shown him. Durril mustered his own life force to consume itself rather than surrender to the ultimate of evils.

Boorgan waited no longer. He had followed Durril, making his way through the death-dealing sea snakes and the frond forest. Injured by his ordeal but determined, Boorgan raced toward the predator.

"Resist, Durril," the loyal companion pleaded. He flung himself onto the Vodyanoi.

Distracted by Boorgan's attack, the Vodyanoi paused in its consumption of Durril to feast on the giant squid's soul. That gave time enough for the wizard to fight back.

Durril threw all his resources into a single spell of exorcism. He focused through the black stone, which began to glow. Shaken by the shift of the magic and the power of the spell, he poured all his ability into the black stone. It burned deep indigo, magnifying the spell. He called upon the power imbued by his master's skull, placing bone against stone.

The Vodyanoi writhed, attempting to expel Durril. The wizard held the beast in magical bondage now. As the stone continued heating, channeling and strengthening Durril's exorcism, the Vodyanoi started to dissolve.

Durril was battered by a chorus of cries of release as each twisted soul found solace in dissolution. He rose and carved a place for himself within the confines of the beast, working outward. If it had not been for the strength of his own master's skull sustaining him, Durril would have collapsed. He did not stop his chant, sending soul after devoured soul to its rest.

The hilt of sword crumbled, unable to withstand contact with the powerful stone. Still the wizard chanted, bringing to his work the honor of the sea nymph Vila, whom he'd not known, and the Lord Chelonia who had shown him the way. He fought against the Vodyanoi long after the magical remnant had vanished.

Durril did not know how long he stood alone in the deep cavern. He gazed transfixed into the perfectly clear crystal resting in his trembling hand, his master's skull clutched to his breast.

Only then did he realize he had triumphed.

Chapter Eleven
✤ ✤ ✤

"THE JURY HAS returned," the ghostly Captain Korrgan informed the anxiously waiting apprentice.

Arpad Zen looked up from his contemplation of the black rocks at the base of the high cliff into Korrgan's face. Sunlight obviously aggravated the captain's pain. The blue lightning had now turned a deep orange as it traced over the ghost's body. All the specters surrounding Zen suffered in a similar fashion.

"Come," Korrgan said. "It is time to face the jury." He led the apprentice away from the cliff's edge to confront the verdict.

"Have you reached a decision?" Korrgan asked.

"We have not, Captain," a tall, wispy, thin specter replied.

"What?" Korrgan cried in surprise.

Zen stared at the jury foreman in wonder. He had expected a death sentence.

"We cannot agree on his guilt," the foreman said. "All except one are in accord, but that one is stubborn and will not be moved," the ghost said in irritation, glaring at the soft-voiced man who had asked Zen his name.

"Let me speak for myself, Segaal," the spirit said, his voice soft in the bright morning air.

"Then speak, Kostane," Captain Korrgan spat.

"I will not take this man's life from him," Kostane said. "It will give us no benefit to have his life. I fully realize"—he stopped the forthcoming protests—"that he was instrumental in many of our deaths. The man sought only to save his own life. There is not one of us here, if he be honest, who would not have done the same thing. Who of us did not so love life that he would have given it up voluntarily faced with Arpad's decision? Not one of us, I affirm."

Silence reigned in the group. Several of the ghosts nodded their agreement with Kostane.

"I remind you of your love for life," Kostane continued, "because you want to take a life now in revenge. That sorry act will not prevent our wandering forever along the beaches, doomed to the pain we suffer this very moment."

"Korrgan's right! We may be doomed, but we will have done something against the cause of our misery," one juror shouted, having had enough of Kostane's reasoning.

Zen stood dumfounded in the midst of the specters. He tried to think of something he could say, something which might sway the group to side with Kostane and let him live.

Kostane spoke again, interrupting the apprentice's speculations.

"Arpad Zen, where is your master?" he asked.

"I do not know," Zen replied. "We were separated in the shipwreck, and Morasha and I were washed ashore here and—"

"Is he alive?" Kostane stopped Zen's verbal outpouring.

"Yes, he is alive," Zen said.

"How do you know, apprentice? You said you were separated from him in the storm," Korrgan asked.

"A master and an apprentice are bonded in a special and secret ritual. I . . ." Zen searched for a way to explain the extraordinary relationship between Durril and himself. He gave up and simply repeated his conviction.

"He is alive! I would know if he were not, just as he knows that I am alive, also."

"Can your master perform an exorcism that will release us?" Kostane asked.

"What are you getting at?" Korrgan interrupted.

"Wait, let him answer," Kostane said. "Arpad Zen?"

"Yes, Captain Kostane. An exorcism would pose no difficulty for my master, Durril," Zen replied, understanding the idea behind Kostane's defense.

"Then," Kostane continued, "our best hope is to aid Arpad Zen, not to kill him. What benefit will we derive if he is a ghost like us?"

"I promise you," Zen said, "I will have my master exorcise you, all of you. It is the least I can do after what I have done for the wreckers."

"What good is your word for your master?" one specter asked, laughing bitterly. "Can any man speak for another, much less an apprentice for his master?"

"It is binding," Zen said earnestly. "I do not make this promise to you lightly. I have given my master's word on this. He will release you as soon as I can find him."

A general hubbub broke out among the ghosts as they debated this new information. The tormenting lightning crawling over their ectoplasmic bodies had turned to a deep bloodred. The group was once again interrupted by shouts coming from the foot of the cliff. This time the shouts were triumphant.

"Oh no, Morasha!" Zen cried as he looked over the edge at the beach below.

Trussed like an animal ready for slaughter, Morasha was being pulled along by the spiteful villagers. Watching from behind stood a contingent of the Wonnean Marines who had captured the unfortunate ogre and delivered her to the chase.

"I must save her," Zen pleaded with his ghostly wardens. "She is my master's familiar. If they kill the ogre body, she will dissolve because there is no one to bind her into another form. She is brave, and clings to life."

"Can you do such a spell?" Korrgan asked Arpad Zen.

"I can at least try," Zen said in rising panic.

"We would all cling to life, brothers, if we could. That is what Arpad Zen did. That is what Morasha strives to do now. For us, our only hope is the exorcism Zen has promised us through his master, Durril. Speak to the question. We haven't much time if we intend to act," Kostane said, goading the spectral crew.

The brutal lightning covering the ghostly

bodies turned a dark purple, lashing the spirits with unimaginable pain.

"Let's go," Korrgan shouted.

As a body, the ghostly crew turned to follow along the headland above the villagers, a grateful Arpad Zen running behind in their wake.

"Kill the ogre!"

"Destroy the beast!"

"It ate my baby! It ate my baby!" one gaunt young woman moaned.

These and other wild cries rang through the dirty, rutted streets of the closely packed village.

"I told you, I told you. The birth of the two-headed calf was an omen, and then the black cat flew past the moon. We must destroy the monster before it destroys us. We must repent!" gibbered an ancient crone, one eye milky-white and twisted in its socket, drool running off her hairy chin.

"Pellas' revenge is upon us, sent to destroy us with this filthy beast!" she said, whipping the crowd to a fever pitch.

"Burn it! We must cleanse our village in the fire!"

Morasha sobbed, shaking with fear. The ogre body had little strength left in it, but she fought as well as she could against the strong ropes holding her. It was no use. She had been almost finished when she blundered into the marine encampment. Seeing the chance of gaining an advantage with the populace, they had captured and bound her, then delivered her to the hysterical mob.

The citizens of the village tore down their

houses and erected a stake, using wood from their miserable hovels for a pyre. Desperately, Morasha sought a form to inhabit, but there were none. All the village dogs had run away or been eaten. No livestock grazed nearby. The peasants starved.

"We will burn the beast sent to devour us," the prophetic crone intoned like a priestess. "When we have destroyed the evil in the heat of the fire, we shall take its flesh into ourselves, destroying its power. We shall overcome the beast and live! I have seen it! I have seen it!" she cried, her blind eye fixed on Morasha.

The ogre struggled in vain. She was hauled to the stake and strapped to it.

"This time the apprentice has really killed me," she thought, wondering where Arpad Zen was.

Angrily Morasha tore at her bonds. Her efforts only resulted in the rough ropes cutting into her already damaged hide.

"Fire, bring the fire!" the priestess-crone ordered. "Bring the fire which will clean our lives and give us strength! Let us live through its death!"

Several lighted torches were thrown onto the pyre at Morasha's feet. Gleefully, the crowd of superstitious villagers danced about their victim, taunting her. One woman held her baby up, dangling it before the ogre's face, laughing.

"You won't eat my baby, monster!" she jeered.

The dry timbers of the village's shacks burned quickly. A pall of roiling gray smoke lifted skyward as flames jumped hungrily toward Morasha. The ogre bellowed in fear, interrupting the manic dancing about the stake. But the familiar mastered herself, desperate to find some way to prevent her dissolution.

She wasn't certain she could die—and she had no desire to find out for sure.

Zen and his ghostly aides peered down upon the village and its horrible rite. The apprentice mumbled, working his hands rapidly, doing his best to invoke the rebinding spell. He knew that he would have no time to release the ogre body from the flames. He only hoped that Morasha could escape and live in another form. Sweat broke out on Zen's forehead as he strained to get the spell right, to make it work. He prayed that he wouldn't fail.

The overwhelming smell of burning ogre flesh assaulted his nostrils as screams pierced the air. The group assembled about the burning pyre went into frenzies of ecstasy, their chants growing louder, punctuated by the tortured cries from Morasha.

"Now," Korrgan said. The ghostly crew flew down the incline into the fire to erupt through it.

Panic reigned supreme among the villagers as the ghostly minions attacked.

Zen finished the rebinding spell and raced toward the burning ogre—too late. There was no way he could get to the familiar through the flames. Even if he could, he held out little hope that the ogre body would live if rescued. All he could do was repeat the rebinding spell again and again.

The villagers ran about screaming, the ghosts chasing them. Everyone attempted to quit the scene except the crone. Focusing her gaze on

Zen, she cackled, as if in a prophetic trance, rallying the peasants to an attack.

"Kill him! Kill him! He would keep us from our feast!" she commanded, pointing a gnarled finger at the apprentice. "Kill him! He has come to destroy us! I have seen the vile tricks of the great Magogh!"

The villagers turned, intent on defending themselves by killing Zen, somehow convinced that his death would rid them of their woes. Against the spectral attack they were powerless. They were caught between the ghosts and their priestess. They attacked. Morasha's ogre body burned on the pyre, sending oily black clouds into the bright blue sky. The stench caused the crowd to gag but not to forget the new object of their wrath.

Zen grabbed a barrel stave. He did his best to fend off the crazed villagers. Kostane appeared beside him.

"Stand firm, Arpad Zen," he encouraged, then disappeared.

The villagers were surrounded by the ghosts as they converged on the apprentice. Fighting with what they could gather as weapons, the specters waded into the crowd, once again breaking its resolve. Soon Zen's attackers were routed, scattered over the countryside.

What had once been the flaming pyre now smoldered, a heap of glowing coals. The ogre body had been consumed.

"Now I've really killed her," Arpad Zen whispered to himself as he stared at the ugly scene. "Oh, Morasha . . ." he began but was unable to finish.

"Arpad Zen." Korrgan called the apprentice's

attention back to his allies. "Arpad Zen, have you saved the familiar?" he asked.

"I . . . I have not, I fear," Zen replied.

"Find your master, Arpad Zen, and return to us," Korrgan instructed. "We will await you on the headland by the beacon."

The ghostly crew disappeared, leaving the apprentice alone in the despicable village. He stared at the funeral pyre and fought to keep the tears from forming. He failed.

Zen left for the beach, seeking the clean smell of the ocean. The day continued in its finery, unnoticed by Zen as he wandered among the rocks along the shore. The spray from the pounding ocean soaked him, washing away the smoke from the awful pyre, its salt blending with his tears. High above, sea gulls cried their bad temper to the cloudless sky. Zen collapsed on the sand, trying to figure out how to find Durril, how to explain Morasha's death.

"I should have known I'd find you lazing about here on the shore in the sunshine when I've been hounded like a rabbit all over this island." A familiar voice chewed at him.

Zen looked up in surprise. "Morasha?" he cried, but he saw only sea gulls basking on the black rocks. "I must be losing my mind," he muttered when he saw no trace of the ogre.

"That would be your excuse. You never could do anything right so now you've decided to get out of it by saying you're losing your mind. Ha!" the voice taunted.

An angry sea gull hopped down from the rock and flapped about Zen's head, battering him with its wings.

"Morasha!" the apprentice cried with joy. "Morasha, is it really you?"

"Of course it's me! And what do you have to be so happy about? It's because of you that I got killed again. If it hadn't been for you, we wouldn't be in this fix," she declared, pecking at Zen's protuberant ears.

"Morasha, you don't have to be so peckish about all this," the delighted apprentice began but gave up in the face of Morasha's continued barrage.

"There you go again. You have no sense of dignity, Arpad Zen, and even less magical ability. Why didn't you help me in the village? All you did was shuffle around and stare at the fire as if you were at a cookout!"

"But Morasha—"

"Don't but me! I don't know why I put up with you. You've killed me four times now. *Four!* I was lucky to find this sea gull's body—it was almost too late, no thanks to you! Although it is much better than that smelly ogre's body."

She stretched her wings, then flapped them as Arpad Zen looked on, biting his tongue.

"And what have you done to find master Durril?" the familiar asked. "What have you been up to, Arpad Zen? Whatever it was," she continued, preventing the apprentice from answering, "I am sure it wasn't trying to help me."

Morasha conveniently forgot the torment she had seen Zen endure in the wrecker's cave.

"Now that I'm free of that awful body you trapped me in, we can set about finding your master. I suppose I will have to do all the work, as usual," she said.

"You haven't even said you are happy to see me, Arpad Zen," Morasha charged.

"But—" Zen tried to get a word in to no avail.

"Of course you aren't happy to see me, anyone could tell that. But you are just going to have to do better. I am sure that master Durril needs our help, and you will just have to do your best to try not to obstruct his rescue. Perhaps I ought to just leave you here," she said.

"Morasha—"

"I can't really do that, since you are his apprentice, although I can't see why he chose you." She glared at him, beady black gull eyes unforgiving. "Speak up, Arpad. What do you have to say for yourself after half drowning me in the sea and then getting me chased all over this detestable island and finally killed?" she asked, barely pausing for breath. Her feathers ruffled and she preened.

"Morasha, I—" Zen attempted to reply before the familiar started in on him again. He wasn't quick enough.

"Never mind. Nothing you could say would make any sense anyway. Get up, let's go! We can't sit around on the beach all day," the familiar instructed.

As he stood, Arpad Zen wondered why he had been so sad at her demise and so happy to hear her haranguing voice. He brushed the sand from his clothes.

"That's better. Now find a boat, if you think you can do it without damaging yourself too much, and let's get going. I'll wait for you down the beach in that little cove where the water isn't so rough."

Morasha took wing, circling gracefully overhead.

"I knew she would blame me," Zen complained to the other gulls perched on the rocks staring at him. "She hasn't changed even if she has a new form," he morosely confided to his feathered audience.

With inexplicable happiness, the apprentice set about finding a boat.

Chapter Twelve
❖ ❖ ❖

"THE VODYANOI IS dissolved," Durril said loud enough for the assembled court to hear.

His news met with a general outburst of disbelief mixed with sporadic cheers.

"I am sad to report that the brave Boorgan gave his life in the effort," Durril continued. "Without his selfless sacrifice, this realm would still be menaced today, and I would not be standing here before you."

"His name will ring in our honor roll of memory along with that of the Lord Chelonia," Rusalka proclaimed. "Your name also shall be honored by us forever, master wizard Durril!"

The sea nymph sat in state on her throne, the royal crown of yellow jewels on her head. She wore a garment of burnished red scales which blended with her hair. The effect of the hair and gown tantalized the wizard. Durril tried to discern what was garment and what was hair against the almost bare, breathtaking, pale body. He failed. She smiled happily at the wizard, her amber eyes sparkling with remembrance of their night together—and promise for more.

"Master wizard Durril," Rusalka said, addressing him with respect before the assembled court, "we are now and always in your debt. Ask of us a victory gift and it shall be yours."

Durril returned the enchanting nymph's smile. He was confident that he had earned his freedom. The black stone from the ancient sword was safely tucked away with Kalindi's blue and red jewels. His master's skull was hidden in the secret pocket recess of the abundant sleeves of his jerkin. All he needed now was one of the yellow stones—and his liberty.

"Rusalka, you are most generous," Durril replied. "Before I take my leave of you, I ask for only the return of my treasure and a small jewel from your crown as a momento. The stones reflect the wonder of your eyes. I would remember them for all time."

Durril bowed low before the sea nymph, an elegant punctuation to his request.

"My dear Durril, a jewel from this crown is a small token for your service. It shall be yours."

True to her word, she removed her diadem and plucked a yellow gem from it, placing it in Durril's eager grasp. Her touch warmed him almost as much as the gem.

"Your treasure, alas, is beyond my ability to return. I am only the guardian of this world's wealth and cannot give it away. What comes to us from the Mother Ocean remains," she refused apologetically, a note of steely inflexibility underneath her explanation.

"We would have you tarry with us longer. There is much we have not discussed," Rusalka said, lowering her dark lashes, "and much to learn from one another.

"Besides," the sea nymph said, stopping Durril's protests, "we must prepare for a victory celebration. This kingdom owes you much. It is at last released from the great evil which has oppressed us for so long. I bid you, go to your rest while we make ready a proper celebration to honor you."

Her eyes told him that she had no intention of releasing him, at least not yet. A few more nights with Rusalka could be pleasurable, but Durril feared she had more in mind than a short time of sporting with him.

Acknowledging her words with another courtly bow, he left the grotto with an escort of marine centipedes. Their deadly ectoplasmic stingers glowed a malicious chartreuse. They comported themselves with proper respect due a hero of rank, but he was certain they were more of a guard than an escort.

He could destroy them with a few words but knew it was better to bide his time. Although he had grown tremendously in his powers, he was still no match for the binding spell the sea nymph used on him.

Back in his quarters, he viewed the entire underwater world using his observation spell. The scrying spell had worked well in the Vodyanoi's maze except for the one desperate time in the monster's cavern. He considered the failure.

There was a blind spot in his sight just as there was a blind spot in his ability to counter the sea nymph's spell over him. Unable to break that grip, he had to cooperate a while longer.

But Durril longed for bright, warming sunlight and the azure of the cloud-specked sky overhead, the bracing, salty breeze against his skin. He wanted to feel the ground solid beneath him and look about through air which did not constantly shimmer, distorting his vision. The wizard hoped Morasha and Arpad Zen were safe and together. He knew they still lived. He thanked the gods that this special bond had not been severed by his tenure under the ocean's waves.

Late in the night, after the honors and the triumphant celebration, and after the salty-sweet wine and the sea nymph had warmed him, Durril lay awake, uneasy. Subtly, he had probed Rusalka's knowledge to find how she had conjured the vortex and the storm. She had been crafty, giving away little, knowing instinctively what he sought. She had been equally demanding, requesting an exchange of magical knowledge, a further physical sharing between them. Durril taught her some elementary tricks to satisfy her demands.

Rusalka was voracious in her desires. She frightened Durril. In her way, she possessed the same greed for power the Vodyanoi had displayed. Whatever the cost, he vowed to keep initiation as a full wizard from her.

She lay at peace beside him, beautiful in the soft rose glow coming from the bacteria clinging to the walls of her sleeping chamber. Careful not to wake her, Durril retrieved his master's skull from his discarded clothing.

He cast a long and thorough observation spell over the sleeping nymph, cloaking it to guard against her detecting the magics even in her slumbers.

The spell revealed a different Rusalka. She was woman and nymph—and something more troubling. She was also an embodiment of the Mother Ocean. He would never be able to fight her in her own realm. The Vodyanoi had once been a creature of the sea. As such, Durril could fight it. Rusalka presented a much different problem.

She was *the* ocean spirit.

Unable to solve this problem, Durril secreted the skull and slept. His awakening was not an unhappy one.

"You are granted the freedom of this realm, master wizard Durril," Rusalka said. "I can do no more. You are too important to us," she said, a wicked smile fleeing across her lips.

"Important to the kingdom or to you, Rusalka?" Durril said, trying to hold his anger back.

"Let us not argue, Durril. Are you not pleased to be here with me?" Rusalka asked prettily.

"You are most charming and beautiful. You are an unmatched pleasure to be with, Rusalka. But my world is above the waves and yours is here beneath the Mother Ocean. We are mismatched and nothing can change that," Durril said, exasperated.

"Your father did not think so when he wed my sister."

"I am not my father," Durril snapped, storming from the stifling chamber.

Immediately, the centipede escort took its position on either side of him. Rusalka had refused to remove them, saying that he must be properly honored. Durril was certain now that she meant properly guarded to prevent an escape.

He mounted an ectoplasmic sea horse reserved for him and left the grotto to ride about the ocean until he calmed down. If he truly had the freedom of the kingdom, he would use it.

His conflicts with Rusalka had been growing. Soon she would not tolerate his polite refusal to teach her all his magical skills. Then what?

Durril spurred the sea horse on, its fiery trail turning a hot blue-white as the sturdy creature increased its speed. The ghostly centipede escort kept pace easily, their distance from Durril just within striking range.

Late that evening, Durril found himself far from the grotto in an unexplored area of the sea. He glanced up and failed to see the surface. He was in deep water. The ocean world lay murky about him with little population to hold his attention.

Suddenly, Durril felt suffocated by the pressing water and the wavering dimness. Imprisonment goaded him to action. A quick movement of his hand and a few pointed words destroyed his escort. Cloaking himself in a protective spell, he spurred the balking sea horse toward the surface.

"If she will not release me, I shall just go," he said aloud to his ectoplasmic conveyance. Durril had carefully probed and found no trace of the sea nymph's sorcery. There was no guarantee he could detect her spells, but it was worth a chance.

The water world brightened as he climbed from the depths. Soon he saw the red glow of a setting sun. With renewed need to be free, he spurred his sea horse mount upward. Then he gasped, his mouth and nose filling with water, his lungs stinging as they reacted to the brine flooding them.

Durril fell from the sea horse. It bolted away, diving back down into the ocean deeps and leaving a burning mark of its passage like a meteor. The wizard strove toward the elusive surface, choking, his chest heavy with the horrible water. The red light from the setting sun which had been so bright now clouded over, darkening more and more as Durril struggled toward it.

Then he was falling, drifting downward, unable to fight the weight of the water. His limbs hung uselessly from his body. His head seemed to burst from the pressure of the insistent ocean. Behind his eyes fireworks burned and exploded.

He had been willing to die, he thought inanely as the Mother Ocean reclaimed him. Then blackness possessed him.

When he came to, an angry Rusalka stood over him. He lay on the white sand before her throne. At first, Durril thought he had died or that he was dreaming. This crazy notion faded. He could breathe, but only in shallow gasps barely deep enough to keep him alive. He fought

constantly to hold back the ever-waiting stran-
gulation of the ocean water.

"How dare you defy me, wizard?" Rusalka
shouted. "Now you will obey! You will teach
me all your spells or you will die, that I promise you!"

"No, Rusalka," Durril croaked defiantly.

Changing tactics, the sea nymph knelt beside
him, a long-fingered hand stroking his cheek.

"You are tired," she crooned in her ancient
lilt. "You will rest in my quarters, and I will
join you soon. Then we can begin my real edu-
cation."

Rusalka dismissed the wizard. He was herded
by two of the red shark beasts to her chambers
where he collapsed, his strength depleted. He
could not take a full breath. A great weight
rested on his chest and he hadn't the strength
to lift it off.

When Rusalka joined him, he bargained for
air. He had to barter for time to find a way to
defeat her.

"I will teach you, but it is an arduous task,
Rusalka. I cannot do it, though, if I cannot
breathe." Durril gasped and sent a trickle of
bubbles from his lips to underscore his difficulty.

Delighted, the sea nymph further released
him. His laboring eased some, but she did not
fully restore him. Proving her supremacy in her
own realm, she reminded him constantly of her
demands.

"Let us begin, master wizard Durril," she said
sweetly, eager for instruction.

"Whatever you say."

He searched among his spells and conjurations for one which would do little damage, one not easily perverted to a dangerous use.

"I shall first teach you how to look at the nature of things," he began. "To see clearly is the basis of all ability. You have to practice this spell until it is perfected," Durril instructed, hoping that it might take her months to command fully.

The wizard complicated the spell, adding extraneous motions and words which did not interfere with the working of it.

Durril broke the spell into parts, although he explained the whole of it to her. She refused to settle for less.

"See that you master each part," he cajoled. "That way your progress will be real and eventually swifter."

The sea nymph was voracious in her quest for magical lore and a quick pupil in spite of the time-devouring obstacles Durril built into the process.

He was able to delay her, though, and to bargain for more normal breathing as a reward for her progress.

In this uneasy manner they passed the days. During the nights the sea nymph instructed Durril.

At last, Rusalka tired of the elementary observation spell. "I am ready for another spell, Durril," she said one morning. "This time, I want the whole of it. That other one was too slow and I grow weary. You do not want to tire me unduly," Rusalka threatened.

"Did I not warn you that the process is a slow one, Rusalka?" Durril countered. "An apprentice spends seven years learning only a handful of simple spells. I readily admit that you are an inspired student," Durril flattered, "but I cannot speed your teaching without fear of missing something important. I do not want to flaw your mastery."

"You will go faster, master wizard Durril," the lovely and determined sea nymph declared. "I have waited far too long for this knowledge. We will move rapidly."

Rusalka did not need to say anything more. Durril felt his breath cut off, the water pressing in on him.

Quickly he nodded his head in agreement and was released to breathe normally again.

"As you say, Rusalka," he said in resignation. "We shall begin next with a spell of transmutation. It is more complicated than the other one, so I beg your patience," he said, wary of her hold over him.

"We will begin. It is important that you employ what you have already learned as a basis for this spell. We shall do something which will delight you. We will teach you to turn shells into gold." Durril saw how this tempted her.

Rusalka laughed, the sound of her joy ringing through the grotto, causing her vassals to turn and look at her in surprise.

"What a wonderful idea, Durril," she agreed happily. "Let's begin!"

Again Durril complicated the transmutation spell, adding much in movement and timing to lengthen the process without altering its effect. Rusalka performed flawlessly, an apt pupil. In no time she had mastered both spells in combination. For a while she remained fascinated with creating gold for her hoard from the debris of the ocean floor. Although disappointed that the gold would not stay transmuted, she accepted the temporary state of her work as part of the spell.

Durril fought hard to keep key knowledge from her. He regretted that he had ever preferred an able and inspired student to Arpad Zen. Now that he had one, she caused his blood to run cold. He walked a narrow path with her.

She began to experiment with the transmutation spell. She tried to magically transmute the more primitive denizens of her realm, giving them a lethal nature. Durril worried that with continued effort, she might succeed. The members of her kingdom sensed her growing power and the mad uses she was putting it to. They became increasingly wary of her. If Rusalka noticed, she did not care. Then suddenly Durril's ruses fell apart.

"Do not attempt to fool me any longer, Durril," Rusalka ordered one morning. "I will have the *real* knowledge now. I would know the exorcism spells and the control spells. I would know your cloaking spell and all the rest."

Durril stood before her as she lounged on her throne. Anger flared from her amber eyes as her red hair billowed wildly around her lush, pearlescent body.

"What do you mean?" he asked ingenuously. Durril attempted to keep calm. This confrontation had come before he had devised a workable escape plan.

Durril had awakened in the night to find her gone. He had waited for her return, drifting off to sleep just before dawn. The glowing red shark escort had unceremoniously pulled him from the resplendent bed to bring him before the angry sea nymph. Only Rusalka and his guards were in the grotto.

"You have been holding back. I would have all the knowledge given to me now," she said, biting the words as she spoke them.

Without allowing him to speak, she continued. "What you have taught me is faulty. You have invented meaningless chants to deceive me," Rusalka said, the old anger and resentment heavy in her voice.

"But—" Durril started to protest. He was quickly silenced by the strangling water, then just as quickly released.

"Quiet!" the sea nymph commanded.

"I have practiced the spells, and I have experimented with them. There is much in what you taught me that is unnecessary. There is much that complicates the process and delays it. You have withheld knowledge that is rightly mine, master wizard, and I will have it now," Rusalka commanded. *"Now!"*

Durril saw no reason to continue the pretense. He drew himself up, ready to face her wrath and defend against it the best he could.

"Never, Rusalka. Not now, not ever will I teach you the lore. The nymph Vila had reason to suspect you. I will not create another wizard to make war on this world," Durril said, bracing himself for the onslaught of the hideous, strangling water.

"We shall see, master wizard Durril," the sea nymph said, an insane gleam in her wrathful eyes. "We shall see."

Chapter Thirteen

✢ ✢ ✢

"WHERE ARE YOU going, Arpad Zen?" Morasha demanded in the squawking sea gull voice she now owned.

"Out to sea. Where else?" the frustrated apprentice answered.

"Out to sea, just out to sea. Don't you have a plan? Of course not. I couldn't count on you for that. I have to do everything," the iliar chided.

Zen steered the small boat toward the treacherous reef. After practicing in the lagoon, the apprentice finally felt confident enough to escape the island. He saw one small, navigable channel. With luck, he hoped to make it through without crashing the tiny craft and dumping them into the water.

Zen was not much of a sailor but he was doing fairly well with the small fishing boat he had stolen. There had been no one around to ask about borrowing the craft. In truth, he would have commandeered it anyway, he was so anxious to quit the awful shores. Now he struggled with the water and the wind and Morasha's constant nagging.

"Look out! We're going to wreck!" she shouted as the apprentice steered for the gap in the reef.

His reaction to her exclamation caused him to start, pulling hard on the tiller. The boat wobbled unsteadily in the water, its sail collapsing as it lost the wind.

"Morasha, shut up!" Zen shouted in return at the truculent gull pouting in the bow of the tiny craft.

"Why don't you fly? That way you won't get wet if I do hit the reef," he growled at her.

The familiar did not answer, recognizing that she had pushed him beyond his endurance. But she did not take wing, either. Morasha sat quietly in the small boat as Zen did his best to find a way to the open sea.

Surprisingly, to Zen as well as Morasha, he got through the narrow channel without mishap. Once outside the reef, the boat moved swiftly out to sea under the brisk breeze. The spirits of both its passengers lifted the farther they traveled from the detestable island and the memories of their misadventures there.

"Well, Arpad Zen," Morasha said, breaking the uncomfortable silence. "What do we do now? Where are you going?"

"I don't know, Morasha," he admitted. "The Mother Ocean is large. Durril could be anywhere."

Morasha fluffed her feathers in preparation for lambasting the apprentice. Zen stopped her. His spirits were revived but still too fragile to withstand much of the familiar's abuse without wringing her neck.

"The best thing to do is for you to go aloft. You can cover more territory that way. Are your eyes keen?"

Grudgingly, Morasha agreed to Arpad Zen's plan. It was a good idea even though she would not tell him so. Instead she responded with a tart reply to his question.

"My eyes are keen, Arpad Zen, no thanks to

you," she added, unable to contain her waspish tongue. "Colors are brighter and clearer. That's no fair trade for losing my fine ogre's body, though."

Zen did not rise to her lack of consistency. She had hated the ogre's body. He leaned back, the tiller resting under his arm. The ocean stretched endlessly in a whitecap-wave-crested green plain. "Then that will be our procedure, Morasha. *You* pick a direction," Zen said, knowing that if they did not locate Durril, he would still be blamed for having gone the wrong way. The apprentice wanted the satisfaction of reminding her that he'd given her the choice in their hunt.

Taken aback by his suggestion, she quickly recovered, replying, "That is wise, Arpad Zen. Knowing you, I am sure you would head out the wrong way."

He did not point out that neither of them knew the correct direction in which to find Durril. The storm had masked the *Pitcairn*'s location well. Instead he agreed to steer wherever she led.

Taking flight, Morasha was soon high above.

Arpad Zen settled into the boat and the comfortable breeze that spelled freedom to him. His master was alive, of that he was certain, and soon they would be reunited. He promised himself that he would pay closer attention and try harder to master the tasks Durril gave him— and without complaint.

The sea moved steadily underneath him like the gallop of a gentle horse. Billowing full in the steady breeze, the craft's brightly striped sail took him rapidly away from the island. Far in the distant sky, he saw Morasha winging in an expanding circle, carefully watching the water for any signs of the master wizard.

A school of playful dolphins accompanied him for a short time. They dove under and around the boat, then through its wake. For a while they raced the craft until tiring of the game. They departed, leaving the apprentice alone with the expansive ocean. For the first time in a long time, he laughed for the pure pleasure of it.

He cleared the barrier islands to the west of Pellas' kingdom and entered the open ocean by midday. Looking back, Zen wondered what the island was called now. To him it could be known by no other name than that of the vengeful king who had damned a man to burn eternally.

Arpad Zen took a deep breath.

"I can see why a sailor takes to a life on the Mother Ocean," he said in contentment to the following wind. For the moment, the terrors of a storm at sea were conveniently forgotten.

Morasha continued to circle high above, ranging before the small craft, then returning to keep it in view. Zen steered to follow her direction, hoping she had chosen the right one. In truth, Durril could be anywhere. How would they ever find him?

Swooping, gliding, Morasha experimented with the air currents and the responsiveness of her new body. The water world twinkled below the familiar with blue and white loveliness. Even the dreadful island made a pleasing pattern from her vantage point high in the clean, cloud-flecked sky.

Zen and the tiny craft formed a colorful dot bobbing on the dark blue-green water. The apprentice had done well negotiating the reef, Morasha admitted to herself, even if he hadn't done anything to help save her life. Burning had been a terrible death. But even Morasha's pouts and her constant state of distress with Zen gave way before the openness of the world which lay inviting all around her.

The gull's body was young and agile. Morasha tested it against the wind currents, now gliding, now winging as she circled. The bird's sharp vision allowed the familiar to examine carefully the moving water for any trace of Durril. She had scanned the small islands as she moved westward. She saw no sign of habitation on them. The wizard was not there.

Morasha had a gut instinct that Durril would not be easily found. Somehow, she did not think that he was a castaway as she and Arpad Zen had been. It would be pure luck if they located the master wizard. She let out a long, anguished bird cry.

All they could do was search and not give up.

The familiar lacked the bonding with the master wizard that his apprentice enjoyed. This did nothing to disturb her firm conviction that Durril lived. Morasha had carefully appraised his abilities on Loke-Bor while inhabiting the dog's body. The wizard was capable and resourceful, and he was quick. Durril lived, she was sure of it. The question haunted her: where might she find him?

Bisecting her circle, then quartering it, Morasha made sure she double-checked each segment. Nothing below her revealed Durril's location. She didn't even know what she sought. Still, the familiar searched, sure she would know a sign of Durril's presence when she saw it.

Moving steadily westward, Morasha noted the storm clouds forming along the distant horizon. She dismissed them as being no obstacle to her search and continued scanning the ocean. She saw nothing below her but deep water glinting in the sunlight. Hope began fading, even as she kept her lonely vigil.

Once she spotted porpoises playing about Arpad Zen's boat before moving off to sport elsewhere. Except for their extravagant gymnastics, nothing broke the surface of the water. A few other adventurous gulls passed her, heading back to the inhospitable island. They squawked greetings and an invitation for her to join them but did not wait to hear her reply.

A swift bank, the force of a rising thermal and Morasha was totally alone in the vastness of the sky. Arpad Zen and the boat had fallen behind, unable to keep pace with her swift flight. She started back to make sure the apprentice kept her in sight.

"It would be just like him to get lost," she groused aloud.

She waited for him, she rested on the wind, spreading her gull wings, stretching and enjoying her strong new body. What a relief it was to be out of the gross ogre body. Morasha laughed and the air filled with the awkward sputtering of gull cries.

The ogre form had been effective on Loke-Bor.

It had been failing badly since becoming physical. Morasha counted herself lucky to be alive. She did two quick barrel rolls in celebration.

The familiar traveled for hours with Arpad Zen following on the sea far below her. She did not deviate from her westward course. Pressed, Morasha could not have explained why she had chosen this direction. Perhaps she would eventually have settled on the traditional lore of the Plenn Archipelagoes as her underlying reason.

West represented the stronghold of evil forces. From the west the old wizards had launched their war. After their evil had ruined the world, they had retreated to the west.

The familiar was convinced that Durril had not escaped difficulty after the shipwreck just as she and Arpad Zen had not. She heeded her instincts.

In the afternoon, the wind picked up, buffeting Morasha and making her flying more difficult.

"The storm is developing faster than I thought," she said to herself, fighting the rough, gusty wind. "If it breaks, we will have a difficult time with the search." She tried not to think of their troubles if they were blown off course.

The familiar beat against the wind, striving to go higher and get above the gusts. Defeated, she turned and sought safety at a lower altitude, hoping that flying would be easier near the water. The storm was gathering its force above.

Morasha got some relief from the tiring wind closer to the ocean's surface. The water had turned choppy. It made her search more difficult. Far behind her, Zen's small craft bobbed willy-nilly on the turbulent water.

"Arpad Zen has his work cut out to control that wallowing fishing boat," she crabbed. "I hope he doesn't get lost out here. Then I'll have to look for him, too."

The familiar made a swooping pass westward and . . . stumbled. Something interrupted her flight, some obstacle which caused her to almost lose control. It was as if she flew into an invisible net thrown into the air in front of her.

Cautiously, she circled to fly the same path again. This time she was prepared for the encounter.

Something physical *was* there. It touched her as she passed over it, entangling her. Morasha reversed direction to fly back through the mysterious barrier. This time she slowed as much as possible without losing the rush of air keeping her aloft.

She brushed across the tips of thousands of thin hairs. They clung like spider webs to her body as she moved past them. Their touch was mildly painful.

Puzzled, the familiar went aloft to think. Arpad Zen made his way toward her, but he had to fight the rising gale. She was sure he saw her, but she still waited for him.

With the coming storm, Morasha was uncertain how long it would take the apprentice to arrive at her location. She wanted him nearby if anything went awry with her plan. He fought his way close enough to the strange invisible obstacle so that she risked the flight into the unseen web once more.

This time Morasha circled about so that she

flew toward the boat. She made her way at a much lower altitude, closer to the ocean's surface. By doing this, she hoped to get some idea of what the thing was when it grabbed at her.

Arpad Zen, she was confident, spied her. If something went wrong, he would rescue her—she hoped.

Morasha slowed her flight, coming in a few feet above the turbulent surface. This time, she opened her mind to Durril. She sought the master wizard with all her magical talents. Morasha called from memory those flashes of unspoken communication she had shared with the master wizard. She relived them. . . .

She hit the barrier's fine, invisible hairs. They quickly withdrew, as if stung. Then just as quickly, but delicately, they raked over her body.

"Durril!" Morasha called, turning to retrace her path, to fly eastward toward Zen.

Delicate tentacles waited for her. They had thickened. For only a brief instant they held her, then gave up their grip, releasing her. The whole of Morasha's new gull body shook from the impact of the master wizard's magical energy.

Morasha beat her way to Arpad Zen and the boat. She thudded into it, making a hard, ungainly landing. Her strength was sapped by the unexpected encounter.

"Morasha!" Zen cried in alarm, releasing the tiller to come to her aid.

"Durril!" she croaked at the apprentice as she flopped about awkwardly. "I found him!"

"Are you sure?" Zen asked, the boat wobbling beneath him.

"Sit down before you swamp us," the familiar ordered, having regained some control over her body. She hopped to the seat and stared up at the apprentice until he settled down. Zen sat, realizing the wisdom of her instruction as water lapped over the side of the rocking vessel.

"It is Durril, Arpad Zen," Morasha reassured him. "He is here, somewhere beneath this stretch of sea."

The familiar paused in thought as Zen struggled to steady the boat in the gusty wind and choppy sea.

"It is strange," Morasha said. "I am not sure what has happened to him," the familiar continued, a worried tone in her voice.

"What do you mean?" the apprentice demanded, once again rocking the boat. Immediately he sat down.

She explained her curious experiences with the web-that-wasn't-there. Morasha assured Zen that without doubt they had located Durril. Neither could figure out what to do about it.

At last, her strength fully regained, Morasha took to the air again. When she returned, her report gave them both slight encouragement.

"Something is down there, Arpad Zen. I think it is a large glass room or a bubble. I can barely see it in this agitated water. The sea is shallower here or I couldn't see it at all."

Both stared into the water, hoping to catch a glimpse of Durril. Their efforts were in vain. It was all Arpad Zen could do to keep the boat in one spot. It had no anchor.

"There is another thing," Morasha said pensively. "The invisible tangle is gone. I flew through where it had been with no difficulty.

Durril must be ensnared in that bubble—and in trouble," the familiar concluded.

"What do we do now?" Zen asked, at a loss as to how to rescue his trapped master.

"How do I know, apprentice?" Morasha snapped, taking her frustration out on him. "Do I have to do all the work? Can't you even solve a little problem like this one? I found him. Durril is *your* master, after all."

Chapter Fourteen

❖ ❖ ❖

"You still refuse me, Durril?" Rusalka asked, angry sparks in her wild honey-colored eyes.

She stood before the master wizard, exquisitely beautiful, her pale skin shining against the golden-scaled garment clinging to her body. Beside her stood a royal coach made from the giant shell of a long-dead chambered nautilus. It was pulled by two powerful, bloodred ectoplasmic sharks.

The sea nymph had partially succeeded in her efforts with the transmutation spell. The sharks' teeth glowed a malevolent green, revealing their newly poisonous nature. Durril wondered if Rusalka found it easier to manipulate ectoplasm than physical substance. If so, her potential for evil was truly horrifying.

From within the confines of his imprisoning

bubble, Durril answered. Distress echoed in his voice.

"I will not teach you, Rusalka. Not now, not ever. You are too dangerous to others—and yourself," the wizard said, again affirming his belief.

"Your life is not worth the sacrifice, master wizard," Rusalka reasoned. "Consider what you are giving up by clinging to a silly principle. Look at the reality of your situation, Durril," she cajoled.

"You're wasting your time, Rusalka. I will not do it. Release me and let me be on my way!" the wizard commanded.

Laughter rang throughout the water world, an eerie sound lacking true mirth. The sea nymph shook her head.

"I give the orders here, master wizard, or have you forgotten? You have had ample time to contemplate my request."

Durril turned his back on her and walked to the far side of his prison cell.

"Very well, Durril. I am patient and can wait for you to change your mind. But do not try my patience too long, wizard. It is not inexhaustible."

Spinning away in anger, Rusalka mounted her chariot and departed, leaving Durril in his solitary confinement.

He did not know how long he had been in the bubble cell. When at last he'd refused Rusalka, she had placed him in the prison and had totally withdrawn his ability to breathe in her underwater realm. He depended on the air supply within the clear bubble surrounding him. He touched its fragile surface and shivered. The soap-bubble-thin wall was all that stood between him and the strangling water.

Each time Rusalka visited him she demanded his knowledge, and each time he refused. She held her wrath in check, but Durril had no doubt that soon she would drown him. If he was to save himself and escape the damnable sea nymph's watery lair, he would have to do something soon. But what?

Again and again Durril reviewed his spells. He called on those of his master's. Luckily, Rusalka had not deprived him of his clothes. He still had his master's skull and the first two jewel components of the spell mirror.

He also had the odd crystal, transformed from the black stone in the ancient sword. He brought it out.

The crystal gleamed in his hand, each planar face catching the dim light, enhancing it much like the room in the Vodyanoi's lair. Durril cast a mild observation spell into the clear stone's depths and saw . . . nothing.

Again he cast the spell—and saw nothing. Whatever the magical stone was, it could not be penetrated by his spell-enhanced sight.

Durril changed his tack. He focused *through* the gem. Without difficulty, he easily espied the bubble surrounding him and the water outside it. He clearly saw the various fish and ectoplasmic remnants that inhabited the area.

Durril employed the power of his master's skull. Drawing on it to sustain the observation spell, he once again attempted to examine the crystal.

"Nothing," he said unhappily.

Durril replaced the skull and the crystal in

the secret pockets of his jerkin. Casting the spells had sapped his energy. Depriving him of air caused him to tire rapidly. He lay down in an attempt to lessen his need.

"I will not be defeated by her," Durril whispered. "I will not teach her. Somewhere there is an answer. There has to be!"

He reviewed all he had learned in the underwater world, finally ending with Lord Chelonia's demonstration and sacrifice.

"That's it!" Durril sat up excited, causing the bubble to bob in the water and tug against its anchor.

"I'll have to employ the life force itself," the wizard said, working out his problem aloud.

Chelonia had used his life force as a last desperate weapon against the Vodyanoi. It had burned itself up, preventing the horror from collecting its power. But that need not be its only use. Maybe there were others. There had to be!

The thought gave hope, and Durril seemed to be out of that fragile commodity. He retrieved the crystal, which concentrated and magnified his spells.

Lying on the floor of his bubble prison, the wizard placed himself in trance. Slowly he called on the life force dwelling within his breast. Gingerly he explored its nature, making sure he did not activate it and cause his own destruction. The tedious effort drained him and he slept, but not without learning something new about himself. A plan slowly took form based on this new knowledge.

"What are you doing now, master wizard?"

Rusalka's demanding voice cut through the wizard's dream. "Are you tired?"

Groggily, Durril fought to claim wakefulness. With difficulty, he sat up and then stood.

The sea nymph stared through the bubble, a puzzled look on her face. He wondered how long he had slept.

She came close enough to touch its tough, flexible surface.

"Durril?" The honeyed tones of the sea nymph's voice wrapped about him. "Why do you torture yourself? Why do you torture me?" she pleaded, promise heavy in her voice.

"This is unnecessary. I do not want to harm you. I would much rather give you pleasure. I offer you this underwater world and its fabulous riches. Together . . . just think of what we can do together, of what we have already done. Say yes, Durril, and I will restore you," she said, finishing her magnificent plea.

Durril fought the lump in his throat that threatened to choke him. He was overcome with a great sorrow and an even greater longing.

Rusalka was more beautiful than ever. She had pulled her burnished hair away from her face and body and held it in place by tiny, twinkling starfish. Her gown of transparent silver scales almost disappeared into the paleness of her bone-white skin.

Durril ached with the desire to say words to please her.

"Come, Durril. Let me restore you to your rightful place beside me. As my consort, anything you ask shall be yours," she crooned, her siren's web wrapping tightly about the wizard.

Durril pressed into the side of the transparent bubble. He could feel Rusalka's hand against his through its thin shield. Her hand was warm, lighting a fire within him.

He started to speak, a heartfelt "yes" forming at the back of his aching throat.

Clutched in his left hand, the crystal burned into his palm, pulling the enchanted wizard back to his senses.

"A spell of compulsion! And cunningly laid on," the wizard thought. Rusalka had grown in ability—almost more than he had believed possible.

Biting his tongue, the salty taste of his own blood filling his mouth with sticky warmth, he choked back the words Rusalka wanted to hear.

"No," Durril said, blood trickling from the corner of his mouth. He wiped it away on his sleeve. "No, Rusalka. *No!*"

Enraged, the sea nymph glowered at Durril. She barely contained her towering wrath. She mastered herself before speaking.

"This is my last warning to you, Durril. I will return at this time on the morrow. You have only one day to reconsider your refusal. What you possess is by right mine! You are valuable to me only so long as you cooperate with me. I will have my inheritance, or I will have your miserable life!"

She stormed off, leaving Durril bereft and desperate in the imprisoning bubble.

"She makes remarkable use of so little knowledge," he murmured. "It is a shame that such talent is so bent toward evil."

Rusalka's nature lay at the core of his refusal to cooperate—and now he faced certain death. Tomorrow Rusalka would, true to her word, kill him. She had waited long enough. If she could not have his knowledge, she would destroy him and have her revenge.

Desperate, Durril clutched his master's skull to his chest. He lay on the floor of his bubble and called on the life force within himself. He had half-formed a desperate plan. Now he had no choice but to use it. Durril focused his full magical powers through the gleaming ward crystal.

The wizard stretched the glimmering essence of himself. Slowly, very slowly he drew it forth from his body until his very soul touched the bubble arching over him.

What Durril did was painful, but he withstood the pain and pushed against the clear, elastic surface. The tendrils of his being stretched until each was an invisible needle. With great care, he pushed them through the bubble's confining membrane into the sea beyond.

A new wave of pain flowed through him. He controlled it, riding it until he became accustomed to the watery world outside his prison. Farther and farther up from the depths, Durril reached with the invisible threads of his being.

A school of small fish swam through those knives of his soul, shooting waves of agony throughout the wizard's essence. Still he persisted, nurturing his life force, thrusting it toward the surface of the water.

As the skein of his being unraveled, Durril fought hard to keep its threads intact. He was torn between the outward thrust and the ease of dissolution. The wizard held on, managing his unusual probing to the world of sunlight and air.

A manta ray swam across his path.

Screaming with indescribable suffering, Durril almost lost his unsure grip on the threads of his life. He pulled back quickly, every nerve in his body singing a song of utter pain.

Durril was almost totally exhausted. What he did required too much energy. Without his master's skull sustaining him and the strengthening of the enigmatic crystal, he could not have continued.

The wizard waited until the waves of stinging pain subsided. Then he pushed outward again across the distance he had lost in his withdrawal. New territory beckoned.

A gentle tickling sensation spread through him, catching Durril by surprise. He had steeled himself against pain. This time he almost lost his hold because of the release from the suffering. The wizard explored the cause of the almost pleasurable sensation.

A group of ectoplasmic kitten-fish romped through his extended being. Their touch set up harmonic vibrations within the stuff comprising the living threads of his identity.

The playful remnants moved on, leaving the master wizard with new considerations.

Durril finally pierced the surface of the water. The touch of air on the tendrils of his essence sent new shock waves through him. He persisted. Numbing himself to this new pain, he extended into the world above the Mother Ocean.

Durril searched for a living body outside the watery world. If he could find one, if he could grasp it, perhaps he could transfer himself into it. Morasha accomplished it through an unknown magic. But if he succeeded, he would no longer be a man or a wizard.

Durril did not hesitate. The familiar's existence wasn't too bad—and he would be alive, free of the sea nymph's dangerous lust for power.

He was willing to chance the transference. In truth, he had no other choice. He liked who he was. He liked his work. He enjoyed his friends. Durril realized that he cared greatly for his apprentice, Arpad Zen. Zen wasn't a quick student, nor was he particularly inventive, but he was good-hearted. The master wizard knew more than ever the value of such a nature.

And there was Morasha, a mystery he had just begun to explore. In a different body, he might not be able to continue his examination of her. He pushed aside the hauntings of his memory. A new—different—body or Rusalka's wrath. Those were his choices.

Durril waited, enduring the pain of his enormous gamble. The threads of his being warmed by the sunlight, he nurtured their fragile essence as he hoped for salvation.

"Ah . . ." He moaned, desperately grappling to hold on to his life force. Ripples passed throughout his soul.

"Something, there is something." Durril rejoiced through his agony.

A second time the tendrils of his being were bruised by the impact of an entity crossing their path. This time Durril sought to understand its nature. It was gone before he could embrace it.

The wizard had reached his limits. If he

probed any farther, he would lose hold of himself and dissolve into nothingness. The tenuous threads of his life force stretched from him like invisible pathways of radiant white light. Durril waited for whatever had passed through the tentacles of his essence to return.

When it came again, it brought shattering pain because it lingered within his grasp.

It also brought hope!

"Morasha!" he cried.

Then she vanished.

Durril concentrated the thin, invisible strands of himself at a point above the water. He brought them together so that they formed a tight bundle.

The impact against his being returned. "Morasha," he called joyfully as she touched him.

There was something physically different about the familiar, but the memory traces she sent could not be denied. What touched him was unmistakably the familiar who had followed and then joined him on Loke-Bor.

Slowly, agonizingly, Durril pulled the threads of his being back. He channeled his life essence until it was encompassed, shielded, guarded by his protecting flesh.

With trembling fingers, Durril pocketed the skull and his crystal. He would survive and Rusalka would be denied the power she wished to corrupt.

Involuntarily, a memory of Hohrman'dur and his perverted fate flooded into the wizard's mind, causing him to tremble. He shook it off, replacing it with one of hope.

"Morasha," Durril murmured, content now in his waiting, assured of his rescue.

Chapter Fifteen

✢ ✢ ✢

"IT IS IMPOSSIBLE," Arpad Zen sputtered, holding to the side of the rocking boat. "I cannot dive that deep."

He clambered aboard the small craft. He fought to bring it back into position over Durril's cell.

"Not that way, apprentice Zen." Morasha's harsh voice followed him. "More to the left. You have to dive again. Master Durril must be freed."

"Morasha, I cannot do it. I have tried four times. The water is too deep. He must be anchored on the bottom. Even if I do reach him, I won't have enough breath to stay and finish the job." Zen growled his frustration at the familiar.

Wind beat at them as the small boat rocked crazily in the water. The storm was building. Soon it would break, and they would be at its mercy with no way to mark Durril's location.

"There is only one solution, Arpad Zen. You will have to kill me," Morasha concluded.

"I can't do that, Morasha," the shocked apprentice responded.

"Why should it trouble you now, apprentice? You've done it easily enough in the past," the familiar said coldly.

"That was different. I didn't mean to kill you. I've told you that. Besides, there is no body for you to inhabit. If I did kill you, which I won't, you would dissolve," Zen said.

"Then you will just have to summon a sea

creature before slaying me," Morasha insisted. "I'd like one of those nice sleek dolphin bodies this time."

"I have never done that summoning spell, Morasha. It wouldn't work," Zen countered.

"Nevertheless, apprentice, you must do it. It is the only way we will rescue your master. Do not tarry. If this storm overtakes us, our chance is lost," the familiar said.

Arpad Zen could not deny the truth of her statements. He felt completely inept. What he did at Durril's raree show bore only the smallest resemblance to what he had to do now. He did not know where any sea creatures swam below, and he did not know how to tell them where he was.

"Arpad Zen, why are you waiting?" Morasha asked.

"I am trying to figure out how to cast the spell. There are problems you wouldn't understand," he said.

At this the familiar laughed, her loud squawks quickly carried off by the wind.

"I understand you are inept, apprentice Zen," Morasha said, "and that you are wasting time."

"Quiet, Morasha. Let me think!"

To his surprise, she did as he asked, sitting with her wings folded, waiting for him to get to work.

The apprentice decided that if he sent out a general summons over and over, keeping the spell going, that he would locate some fish or other. It was the best he could do. Zen was not sure he could call a dolphin, as Morasha desired. He hoped one would come, because if she ended up as a spiny, mottled toadfish he would never hear the end of it.

Briefly he explained to Morasha what he would try. She nodded her agreement.

"Hurry, we have wasted enough time and effort already," was her only comment.

Zen fought the wind and the boat. He chanted, sending his magical summons into the watery world.

"Nothing is happening," Morasha complained, scanning the water. "What is wrong?"

He did not answer. All his concentration went into the summoning spell. But the apprentice was disappointed, too. Something should have responded to his call if the Mother Ocean was as populous as was commonly believed.

Finally he stopped chanting, accepting the truth of his failure.

"Why have you stopped?" the familiar demanded.

"It isn't working, Morasha. The spell is too general. I have nothing to focus it on. Somehow, the water disperses and weakens it." Zen fumbled in explanation.

"I knew I couldn't count on you. Why Master Durril took you as an apprentice is beyond me," she said.

A thick, unhappy silence hung between them. The rocking boat made Arpad Zen queasy. He looked at the roiling ocean surrounding him and sickened.

"What is wrong with you now?" Morasha asked as she watched Zen's face take on a pale greenish countenance.

"I am getting seasick," he said.

"You can't do that now, of all things! You

can't indulge your frailties just because the water is a little choppy," she cried, forgetting her own debilitating time on the *Pitcairn.*

"I will just have to go aloft and find something. I knew you would have me do all the work again—as usual."

Morasha took wing against the strong wind to search for some form of life. Zen was left to his misery in the small boat. He had to fight his own stomach in addition to the water and the wind. The apprentice held to the spot in spite of the difficulties assailing him.

When Morasha returned ten minutes later, she thudded into the boat with happy news. Her awkward landings were part of the gull's flying style.

"That way." With a wing, she pointed east. "They are that way. There are several dolphins. The group is some distance from us. This time, Arpad Zen, you *must* make them come to us. It is our last opportunity to save Master Durril."

The apprentice gathered his strength, suppressing the nausea which threatened to overwhelm him. He started chanting the summoning spell again. This time he sent it in the direction of the dolphins. Realizing that the familiar was again correct in her estimation of their situation, he gave up trying to control the small craft and concentrated solely on the spell. Zen added a compulsion spell to its casting. The irritating itch of working magic crawled over his body. Arpad Zen redoubled his efforts.

Morasha went aloft to supervise. She swooped by several times, calling encouragement.

"One of them is coming," she shouted as she flew off to monitor the dolphin's progress.

Zen set his full concentration to the spells, doing all he knew how to strengthen their pull.

Within a minute, he saw the graceful leap of the dolphin as it swam rapidly toward the boat. Morasha thumped down beside him. Feathers scattered everywhere from her clumsy landing.

In no time the chattering animal pulled alongside the rocking craft. It continued to play about the boat as Zen held it with his call.

For once, Arpad Zen dared to hope.

"Who dares tamper with my realm?" Rusalka asked, interrupting her practice of the transmutation spell.

The sea nymph angrily cast about, trying to pinpoint the source of her irritation. A weak, erratic magic clawed at her.

"Someone interferes with the creatures in my domain," she said, mounting her chariot.

The red sharks moved swiftly from the murky depths of Rusalka's secret room where she refined her powers in private. She returned quickly to the seat of her authority in the grotto.

Without delay, the sea nymph placed the yellow-jeweled crown on her head and sat on the throne.

"I will not permit it," she said to her guard of deadly, innocent-looking flatworms. They stirred in anticipation. She waved them to their positions. She would deal with this feeble intrusion personally.

"Power of storm . . ." Rusalka called as she sought out those who offended her.

The sea nymph entered a deep trance, com-

bining her will with the natural forces of the
storm to focus its wrath on whoever she chose.
She was completely vulnerable, lacking con-
scious connection with those about her.

The sea nymph completed her spell. She released the storm, pinpointing its attack on those
who disturbed her.

"They are near Durril's confinement bubble,
Voiyah," Rusalka said to one bloodred shark.
"Go. Find out what is happening. Take Yahnoy
with you. Do whatever you like if something attempts to disturb the wizard's imprisonment,"
she crooned.

"Make haste!"

Darting from the sea nymph's grotto, the
ghostly twin monsters hurried to fulfill her
wishes.

The beautiful underwater palace had
changed. No longer did sea life frolic there. All
that remained were the pearlescent ghosts silently guarding the immense hoard which lit-
tered the floor—and Rusalka's death-dealing
guard.

"Before I kill him, I must retrieve the stone
from my crown," she said, her small hands
drawn into possessive fists.

"I *have* to kill him. But I am learning, my
pets. I have you now. I haven't the need for Durril I had previously."

The flatworms pulsated an alarming violet in
response to the sea nymph's praise.

"What could Durril have wanted with one of
these stones?" she asked the unresponsive
worms as she fingered her crown. She frowned
as memories flooded her.

"Vila insisted on having a diadem of these unimportant gems," Rusalka confided to her guard. "My sister was led astray in many things by her lover. I will see that a new crown is made, one befitting a real queen of this realm."

"Now, apprentice Zen. You must kill me so that I can enter the dolphin's body," Morasha demanded.

"Morasha, I . . ." The thought of purposely killing the familiar appalled Arpad Zen. He carried too much guilt from his prior accidental killings of her. His life would be more pleasant without her, he had to admit—but he could not willfully take her life.

"Come on, Arpad Zen, transfer me to the dolphin! The storm is coming."

"Wait, Morasha, I have to start the rebinding spell or it won't work. You will dissolve." Zen stalled, unable to think of anything to dissuade her.

"I transferred to this gull's body without your help," she said. "You can never be depended on for the least little thing."

"But I chanted the rebinding spell above the village and once again when you were tied to the stake," Zen protested. "I don't think you can change forms without it. At the time I didn't know it had worked. That's why I was so surprised to meet you on the beach. And then you wouldn't let me explain . . ."

Zen's protests gave Morasha only brief pause. She ignored what the apprentice said. To acknowledge it meant that she would be indebted to him for saving her from the murderous villagers. Instead, she attacked him.

"Arpad Zen, get on with the spell before the

dolphin leaves us. Do you want to rescue your master or not?"

"All right, all right. Give me some time," he said as he reviewed the steps of the spell.

After he conjured a weak holding spell to keep the dolphin near, the apprentice gave full concentration to the rebinding spell. Again his skin crawled with the itch of a working magic.

"Are you ready?" Morasha asked impatiently.

Zen nodded his assent.

"Then kill me," she said.

"Please, no!" he exclaimed.

"We have just been through this whole thing, apprentice. You *must* kill me or I cannot change form. Don't you understand even that basic relationship?" The familiar spat. "Now do it and don't botch it!"

"Can't you just drown yourself?"

"Of course not, Arpad Zen! This gull's body would not willingly destroy itself. I have no control over its basic nature. *You* must do it, apprentice," the familiar said, great impatience reflected in her words.

Hesitantly, Zen gripped the strong gull's body. His hands shook. Everything he had done to Morasha had happened because of his ineptitude. Now, faced with her willful destruction, he trembled. The gull warmed his hands. He felt its frightened heart beating, the rhythm of its hurried breath.

"I can't do it, Morasha," he cried, releasing his hold.

Morasha fell to the bottom of the boat with a loud thump.

"Ouch! You clumsy oaf! What do you think you are doing?" the familiar demanded.

"I just can't kill you, Morasha," Zen said.

"There you go again, making excuses." Morasha scolded him, fixing Zen with her bird's cold black eye. "This is the *only* way to save your master, and you sit there quibbling."

"There must be some other way," the apprentice protested.

"What?" Morasha demanded.

"Well . . . you could take to the air and somehow measure the distances to this place. Then, when the storm is over, we could bring a crew, and—"

"Arpad Zen, wring my neck!"

The apprentice closed his eyes and grabbed her. Quickly, he did as Morasha commanded. She was right and he was wrong. The fragile neck popped as he twisted hard. Her free-floating pink spirit rose from the dead bird lying broken in his hands.

Zen stared at it. How many times had he wanted to wring Morasha's neck? Now he had done it, and he was not happy.

Pink ectoplasm hovered over the gull's remains, then started to stretch, thinning out to float on the gusty wind.

The apprentice chanted the rebinding spell as the dolphin passed about the boat. Chattering, the curious animal lifted itself out of the water to dance on its tail as it looked at the pink remnant floating above.

Striking with all its fury, the storm almost tossed Zen out of the craft into the angry water. It lashed at him and his weak magical hold on Morasha's spirit.

He clung to the fishing boat's small mast, chanting as Morasha's ectoplasmic substance whipped about on the howling winds, lifted high above the water.

Zen faltered as panic overtook him. He began the chant again but confused its activating elements as water lashed over the side of the wobbling boat, almost drowning him.

"I'm losing her," he moaned.

High-pitched squeals emanated from the dolphin as it fought the hold Zen had placed on it. Zen's grip on the beast slipped just as his rebinding spell on the familiar slipped, also. Desperate, he struggled to balance the two spells. Water and wind slapped at him, knocking him about the boat.

"Morasha!" he called in alarm. The pink ectoplasm was drifting away from the vessel, trapped by the high winds.

The apprentice closed his eyes. Kneeling in the middle of the storm-tossed boat, he began the rebinding spell once more. This time he pronounced each word slowly, carefully, taking time over the sequence and rhythm of the spell. He focused it, channeling it toward the dolphin tugging with increasing success at his weak spell of compulsion.

Howling storm winds beat the water, whipping it into great white-crested waves. They battered the tiny craft. Lightning flashed overhead as dark clouds opened, delivering their heavy burden and almost swamping the boat.

Zen did not give up. He clung to the side of the vessel as it was tossed about the Mother Ocean. An offending wave lifted the small boat high into the air, then slammed it down again. Zen lost his grip. He fell back against the mast, hitting his head.

". . . one substance!" he gasped in conclusion before losing consciousness.

Chapter Sixteen
✛ ✛ ✛

"OH!" MORASHA GASPED.

She moved swiftly. A loud chittering of distress assailed her. She leaped from water to air, then dove into water again, turning to leap and dive once more. Several times Morasha passed from the watery domain into the rampaging storm and back into the water.

Spread thin by the storm wind, her essence on the verge of fragmenting, the familiar's agony was swamped by another pain like a sharp blow.

"Shir-raz! Shir-raz!"

The words of panic beat at Morasha.

"It has come, and I must die while there is still time," the crazed voice lamented.

"Where am I?" Morasha asked, shaken by the fear surrounding her. Never before during a rebinding spell had she felt out of control, in a frenzy.

It was the frenzy of a physical body in extreme distress.

"Shir-raz! I must die!"

Diving deep, Morasha felt air forced out of the body she now inhabited. Then something different and frightening flooded in. It hurt. It suffocated her.

"Water!" Morasha shouted. "I'm drowning! Stop! Stop now! I will not harm you," the familiar pleaded.

"Shir-raz, I must die!"

"No, stop," the familiar commanded. "I am not Shir-raz. Do not die. Please."

Morasha did her best to convince the frightened dolphin that she meant no harm. The rebinding spell had worked—but the dolphin was killing itself. Delicately, Morasha withdrew as much as she could from the alarmed beast. She did her best to soothe it.

"Please," Morasha begged. "I will explain. Go to the surface. Do not die. I will not harm you."

"What are you?" an hysterical voice demanded, cut off by the choking water.

"I am *not* Shir-raz. Please, we must survive!" Morasha begged. She experienced the awful weight of the ocean and the body laboring for breath.

"No. Shir-raz! Only by dying can I stop it!" the dolphin answered. "The elders instruct us. When Shir-raz comes, we must die. Only through death can we stop it using us!"

"I am not Shir-raz," the familiar replied, forcing herself to calm down. "I am Morasha, and I want you to live. Please, hurry. You must live!"

Morasha pulled away as far as possible from the dolphin's consciousness. The familiar bundled herself into the smallest knot of energy possible, giving over to her host all control of its being. She opened herself, trying to show the dolphin she meant no harm, that she would not hurt it.

Whether by Morasha's efforts or its basic instincts for survival, the frightened beast labored toward the surface and the life-giving air. Once there, it demanded again, "If you are not Shir-raz, what are you? What do you want?"

"I . . . I am Morasha, the master wizard Durril's familiar," Morasha explained. "You must be the dolphin we summoned." She struggled to find the proper words.

"Arpad Zen, the master Durril's apprentice succeeded in casting the rebinding spell," the familiar tried to explain.

"Arpad Zen? Is an Arpad Zen the clumsy one on the water? The storm has sent it away. Look."

As Morasha leaped from the sea into the storm, she scouted in all directions through the dolphin's eyes. Arpad Zen was indeed gone, swept away by the winds and the turbulent sea.

"What is Shir-raz?"

"We must die if it comes," the dolphin replied. This time Morasha realized that the sleek, powerful body she inhabited was young, at the beginning of life.

"Please, do not be afraid. I am not Shir-raz. You must live," Morasha soothed.

"Our lore tells of Shir-raz. When it comes, there is little time. If we do not want to become something . . ." The dolphin faltered, then began again.

"The only way we can prevent becoming something evil is to die immediately. The elders tell us that we have only a little time to fight

Shir-raz or it takes us. So we are taught to die. No one has been taken by Shir-raz in a long time, but we are still taught to die rather than let it have us."

Morasha realized the frightened animal was speaking of some remnant from the Spell Wars. She was amazed that the dolphins recognized the threat and had devised a way to fight against it.

"Leave me now. Your presence is quite painful!" the dolphin requested.

"I am sorry," Morasha said, stunned by her unique situation. "I do not believe I can leave."

"You can't leave?"

The loud chittering started again as the dolphin circled about, verging on panic, shaking its head in an attempt to dislodge the familiar.

"Believe me, I *am* sorry." Morasha sought to calm the fearful animal. "This has never happened before. I think we are bound to one another until I can free the master wizard Durril. He will unbind us," Morasha assured the dolphin.

"Please forgive me," Morasha begged, seeing that the dolphin refused to be soothed. "And please calm down. I won't hurt you, I promise."

The dolphin ceased its frenzied movement. It still swam in a wide circle, occasionally leaping into the raging storm as if to check its progress.

"Why are you here? What are you? What do you want?" the dolphin asked, its uneasiness apparent.

"I will explain," Morasha said. "I need your help. We must work together. I need the use of your body, and there is not much time!"

Morasha tried to convey her need for immediate action to the young dolphin.

Eventually Morasha gained the dolphin's grudging consent.

"I am called Saemo," the dolphin finally said by way of hesitant greeting. "I will help you because I have little choice. You must swear to leave me as soon as you can. I am very uncomfortable," Saemo said, finally accepting her unusual condition.

"I promise, Saemo. Had I known this would happen, I would never have had Arpad Zen summon you. I've inhabited many bodies but never have I shared intelligence. It does not appeal to me. Please understand that my need is desperate and that our circumstances cannot be immediately changed." What other argument might persuade? Morasha had no experience in such matters.

"Also, I must ask you to turn the control of your body over to me," Morasha began.

The familiar felt panic rising once more in her hostess. She spoke quickly to reassure her.

"Please, Saemo, I will return it to you. I want out of your body as much as you want me out. I must be in control of the body to complete my task. After it is done, I will return control to you until Durril can figure out a way to separate us."

Morasha did not mention that the only way she had ever managed to change bodies before was through the death of her host. The dolphin was a highly intelligent being. Already the familiar greatly respected Saemo and her kind. Morasha did not want the dolphin killed to achieve her own release.

Before any solution could be found to this dilemma, the familiar had to free Durril.

"There is little time, Saemo. I must act quickly to save the master wizard Durril or all is lost," Morasha begged.

"Very well," the dolphin said. Having reached a decision, Saemo gave control of her body to the familiar.

At first, Morasha wobbled in the water. She was soon able to connect herself to the dolphin's body as she had in so many of her past forms. It was a fine, strong vehicle. She was aware of Saemo nervously waiting, holding back. The familiar did her best to soothe the unfortunate being whose shock and unhappiness at sharing a body was a feeling Morasha agreed with.

Expertly, Morasha leaped out of the water, breathing deeply. The angry storm raged about her. Then she plunged into the Mother Ocean, diving rapidly toward Durril's prison cell.

The familiar sent out high-pitched sounds which rebounded in the underwater world to give her explicit directions.

"What an excellent way of finding your way," she thought.

"Thank you," came a brief comment from Saemo, who then hesitantly withdrew.

Morasha located the wizard. Had she been seeking him with her eyes, the familiar would have been totally lost in the pitch-black world. With sound images, Morasha gained a clear picture of the imprisoning bubble. She quickly pinpointed the anchoring device.

As she explored it, her keen senses detected the approach of Rusalka's shark troops.

Before the two ectoplasmic killers could close on her, Morasha adeptly twisted away, turning rapidly to ram them. A powerful flip of her tail sent her rocketing forward, nose tensed for the killing blow.

She passed through them. Their gelid substance cloying, Morasha slowed and tried to think of a new attack. Had they been physical, the familiar would have easily injured, perhaps killed them. But the two deadly beings were modified remnants of the Spell Wars. As such, the dolphin's defenses against true sharks were useless. Morasha felt Saemo trembling in the background of her consciousness, but the dolphin did not interfere.

Morasha did not give way. She circled Durril's bubble, coming up under it to ram again through the deadly sharks. This time the ectoplasm chilled her.

One gave chase as the other remained on guard by Durril's bubble cell.

The shark remnant was almost as fast and agile as a dolphin—almost. Morasha did a quick roll, twisted and dove through her foe a third time. The familiar could not maintain the attack much longer. Their touch would eventually paralyze her.

Recovering slowly, she sped back to the wizard's bubble. Her ectoplasmic assailant was discomfited for only an instant before it gave chase.

"Durril? Durril, can you hear me?" Morasha called.

"Yes," the wizard said, surprised to see the familiar in dolphin form.

"Here," she cried. "Just beyond the bubble!"

"Morasha! I knew it was you!" He pressed against the membrane, his face distorted by its filmy substance.

Morasha sped around the bubble, then turned upward just before colliding with the bloodred shark remnant, barely missing its poisonous fangs. Her pursuer collided with its mate.

"Morasha, swim about my cell, if you can. I must ward you," Durril said.

The familiar did her best to stay close to the bubble. It was a difficult task. She circled the bubble in almost every direction, twisting and turning frantically to avoid the deadly chase of the ectoplasmic hunt.

Durril worked to send a warding spell through the tough skin of his prison cell. He focused the spell through the crystal, magnifying it, shaping it, guiding it. The wizard had an odd sensation of delay, and partial loss, but he was confident that the spell was having some effect. He kept chanting, repeating it in a continuous effort to protect the familiar.

"What is that?" Saemo asked, horrified, as the tingle of magic crawled along the skin of her sensitive body.

"Protection!" Morasha yelled, rolling away from one ectoplasmic shark to charge around the second.

"I don't like it!"

"Do not interrupt," Morasha commanded, "not if you value our lives!"

Saemo's interruption had broken Morasha's concentration. She came close to being raked by the shark's vicious teeth. If their hot poison touched her, both the dolphin and she would die horribly.

Morasha was not fully prepared for the savagery of the next attack by the bloodred horrors. They charged, one from below and one diving from above. With graceful agility, she turned to avoid contact—but not quickly enough. Her flipper brushed against the deadly teeth.

Morasha watched the venom burn along the edge of her flipper and then dissolve, doing no damage.

Durril had completed the warding spell! Encased by it, the dolphin familiar was temporarily safe from the ectoplasmic evil which sought to kill her.

"Morasha," Durril called. "Can you free me?"

"I do not know," the familiar answered, once again circling the bubble with the spectral sharks in close pursuit. She turned unexpectedly, ramming into them. This time, they recoiled slightly from the touch of the magics surrounding her.

Durril struck at the predators through the bubble, but his spell was delayed just enough for them to escape it. He tried again, sending a spell of exorcism after fixing their deepening-red bodies with the observation spell. They moved too rapidly for success.

Again the familiar rammed the shark remnants, natural dolphin instincts working against the shark menace. Durril noted the small effect the warding magics had on them.

"Morasha," he said, "stay close. I want to cast another spell. While I am doing it, you must not ram the sharks," the wizard ordered.

"I will try, Master Durril, but hurry. This dolphin's body is tiring rapidly. I do not know how much longer I can keep away from them.''

Once more Morasha circled the bubble, easily avoiding the anchor, having more difficulty eluding the sharks.

The predators sensed what Durril attempted. They struck at Morasha, driving her away from the wizard's cell. Stubbornly she dodged them, returning to circle the bubble.

Durril chanted. Holding the crystal before him in his left hand and his master's skull in his right, the wizard laid a honing spell along the dolphin's body.

Durril felt a fleeting contact with the familiar. Somehow that tie helped draw his aid to her. Durril created a cutting edge of supreme power like the one he had placed on a well-sharpened sword at the Valley of the Ultimate Demise.

It was slow, difficult work. Morasha had to move constantly and swiftly to avoid death. The bloodthirsty predators frequently blocked her from Durril's line of focus, interfering with his building of the hard, thin destructive edge.

Several times he thought he had lost her as the familiar was chased from the scene. Each time Morasha fought back.

At last it was done.

''Now, Morasha!'' Durril commanded. ''Now, cut through them!''

The wizard gave the order just in time. The larger of the monsters dropped on her from above.

Twisting adroitly, the familiar lunged away. Tiring, her turn for an attack faltered, but she recovered. Morasha gathered speed and rammed into the ectoplasmic beast. This time the magics surrounding her burned into its bloodred substance. Startled, the shark lurched away as it emitted a scream of ghostly pain.

Morasha circled to swim with full force into her second pursuer. This time she passed through it, the effects of Durril's honing spell burning into its ectoplasm like lightning from one of Rusalka's mighty storms.

Morasha became the pursuer. Taking the offensive, the familiar attacked. She passed through both predators. Substance severely diminished, they turned tail and swam frantically. Morasha chased them only long enough to be sure they would not return, then hurried back to aid Durril.

"Well done," the wizard said.

"Thank you, Master Durril," Morasha replied.

"Yes, Morasha, very well done," Saemo complimented her visitor. The familiar acknowledged her hostess, then spoke to Durril.

"If you will stand aside, I'll ram this bubble and free you." She swam around, readying herself for the attack.

"No, Morasha!" Durril exclaimed. "That means my certain death."

He could almost feel the suffocating water flooding over him, filling nose and mouth and lungs.

"I cannot breathe if you break the bubble. Can you detach it from the anchor? It'll float to the surface if released."

Morasha did as instructed. She inspected the device holding the prison cell to the ocean floor. The chamber was held by thousands of filaments protruding from large, barnacle-encrusted rocks. Gingerly, Morasha touched them with her nose. An irritating tingle surged along her body, causing her to jerk back.

On closer inspection, she saw that the filaments were extrusions from a colony of mutated clams. As she sounded them, their vibrations showed an unpleasant, stinging orange to her new sight.

She touched them again, this time with more force. Ready for the smarting surge, Morasha found that it annoyed more than it harmed. The filaments stretched under the pressure of her attack. They were strong and elastic, but enough pressure would break them.

Morasha measured the anchor. There were only a few feet between the shells of the clam colony and the tough filaments connected to Durril's bubble.

The familiar moved away from the anchor and the wizard's bubble. She swam some distance and then turned, sending out sharp exploratory sound waves which returned to her a clear picture of the bubble and its anchor.

Morasha climbed toward the surface. Pirouetting on her tail fins, she dove downward at the offending filaments as fast as she could, hoping that her swift passage would rip them apart.

As she hit the mass of extrusions, firelike tendrils crawled along her body, stinging it in spite of the warding spell. At first the filaments only stretched, causing a brief moment of panic. Then they snapped, one after another, releasing secondary waves of burning fire around her body. Because of Durril's spell, Morasha was

not really harmed although she was uncomfortable.

Morasha broke the filaments' grip. Durril's
imprisoning cell began to slowly rise. The familiar turned to follow. The bubble gained
speed as it neared the surface.

Durril could not keep his footing inside the
spherical prison. The free-floating chamber
spun, tumbling him around like a pebble caught
within a drum.

The bubble erupted onto the surface of the
Mother Ocean, only to be taken by the sea
nymph's storm and carried away.

When Morasha reached the surface, Durril
was nowhere to be found.

Chapter Seventeen

✤ ✤ ✤

"MASTER DURRIL!" MORASHA called forlornly,
her words lost in the wind of the sea nymph's
fierce storm.

The familiar jumped frantically from the water, scouting in every direction. After her battle
with the shark remnants and the unsettling experience of sharing a body with another intelligence, losing Durril was too much for the
familiar.

"Morasha," Saemo interrupted, calming her
guest. "He cannot be far. Let's look with what
we hear."

Saemo helped Morasha focus on the echoes surrounding her. Morasha's panic subsided. The familiar began the purposeful search for Durril. From far off, a group of high-pitched squeals told her that other dolphins were in the vicinity.

"They have come looking for me," Saemo explained. "Let's ask them if they see the bubble."

Morasha and Saemo enlisted the help of the other dolphins who soon located the wizard adrift in his bubble. Durril motioned to them that he could not free himself. The waves tossed him about, making him lose balance inside the sphere. The dolphins swam closer, then attacked the prison cell. Morasha delivered the final blow with her snout. She popped the bubble, dropping Durril into the Mother Ocean.

"Quick, Master Durril, take hold," the familiar said as she swam beside him.

"Morasha? How did you end up as a dolphin?" Durril asked.

"It's too long a story. I will explain later when there is time. Now we must find Arpad Zen," Morasha said. "He was swept away by the storm when I dove to locate you."

The wizard mounted Morasha's slick dolphin body, grateful for such fast transportation.

"Do you have any idea where Arpad has gone?" Durril asked.

"Arpad Zen never does anything right," Morasha complained. "He probably went back to that detestable island we were on. If I never see it again, it will be a year and a day too soon!"

The familiar's grumpy accusation did not hide her underlying concern. Durril laughed but was also taken aback by Morasha's worried petulance. He hadn't realized she cared so deeply for Zen.

"Then let's get going. He may need help."

The wizard invoked a strong cloaking spell as protection against Rusalka's detection. Morasha and the other dolphins swam toward Pellas' island, Durril riding with them. Two of the group scouted ahead and sent word that they had located a small craft with a being in it which might be Zen. The familiar increased her speed, making rapid progress toward the vessel.

When they drew alongside the rocking boat, the apprentice was hanging over the side, nausea having finally mastered him. He definitely looked the worse for riding the storm-tossed water so long. Turning dull eyes toward them, he tried to speak. Only weak choking sounds came from his puffy lips. Zen swallowed hard and tried to focus his eyes.

"We might have known you'd head this way. Can't you keep out of trouble? And of course, I would have to find you after barely rescuing Master Durril when you didn't stay to help," Morasha said.

Seeing the familiar helped him recover from the seasickness. "Morasha! You are alive —the spell worked. I made it work," the apprentice crowed in unabashed delight, ignoring her chiding and forgetting his illness.

Then he grabbed his head. The blow against the small mast had raised a large bump and hurt when he yelled.

"And Master Durril, you are rescued. I didn't think we would find you. If it hadn't been for Morasha, we wouldn't have, and then the storm came up and we had to fight it and I had to wring Morasha's neck after she had become a sea gull," Zen blurted out in relief, his joy obvious at having the wizard back with them.

"You did well, Arpad," Durril said, smiling. "I am most happy to be back with you, also, believe me."

Morasha pulled close to the small vessel. Durril climbed aboard, legs hurting from lack of use in his cell. He checked Zen's bump, clucked professionally a few times and administered a simple healing spell.

The dolphins romped close by as the three companions tried to figure out a plan.

"We have to go back to the island, Morasha," Arpad Zen said. "I gave my word. I promised them, Master, that you would exorcise them. The dead sailors are waiting for us." He swallowed hard and rubbed the spot Durril had conjured.

"My promise is the only reason they did not kill me. And they helped me rescue Morasha from the villagers," he finished.

The familiar chittered at Zen, a dolphin laugh. "You didn't save me. You killed me," she accused.

"I managed to properly cast the rebinding spell, or you couldn't have become a sea gull," he said self-righteously.

"Enough." Durril interrupted what looked to be an unending argument. "We won't get far with the two of you fighting like this. The storm has blown itself out. We will return to the island. Arpad has given my word and in good cause, I think."

The apprentice quietly basked in his master's slight praise.

"Oh, very well," Morasha said with ill grace. "Thank Croy for this nice dolphin's body. I won't have to go onto that horrible shore again."

"Perhaps none of us will," Durril said. "I have no desire to deal with the Wonnean Marines. We can maneuver this craft to a location opposite the lighthouse. I can work from there."

"There is something else, Durril," Zen began.

"Master Durril," Morasha corrected.

"There is something else, Durril," the stubborn apprentice continued, ignoring Morasha's correction.

"The lighthouse . . . it is powered by the burning ghost of a damned man. I couldn't exorcise him so I transmuted him—I tried to transmute him. Tukker was going to have Trevoor kill me if I didn't stop him from burning—the ghost, not Trevoor—and I couldn't think of anything to do. I tried the transmutation spell, the one you use for the raree show, but I couldn't make lead into gold because there was no lead. I didn't really want gold anyway, so I tried to make fire into water but I got only mist—"

Durril broke into a laughter of true happiness which stopped Zen's flood of words.

"Now see what you've done," Morasha snapped angrily at the apprentice for no apparent reason.

"I haven't done anything, Morasha," Zen said, confused.

"Please, Arpad, finish your story," Durril said when he had recovered.

"Finish my story?" the apprentice said in

surprise. Seldom did his master *want* to hear any of his tales. He did not tarry in the telling.

"I was able to transmute the burning ghost to mist for longer periods of time. The wreckers were happy with that for a while because the ships crashed on the shore like they wanted, like the wreckers wanted. But I couldn't make the ghost dissolve. He still endures the pain," Zen said, warming to his tale.

When he'd finished the damned man's story, and the telling of his awful experiences with the phantom sniffer hound, both Durril and Morasha said nothing for a while. Then the wizard stroked his chin and came to a decision.

"If the marines are on the island, they will care for the light. They will not allow harm to come to any vessel passing through these straits. I will exorcise the burning ghost, also," Durril declared, much to Zen's relief.

"Now, let's get close enough to the shore so that we can work. And Arpad, you've done well. You've done *very* well," the wizard said.

His apprentice blushed a bright pink. Privately, Durril reviewed his opinion of Arpad Zen. Morasha said nothing, which for her was most unusual.

With some effort, Durril and Zen managed to get the boat opposite the lighthouse without crashing into the reef. Evening was descending on the Plenn Archipelagoes. Morasha was content to be with the dolphins. She seem preoccupied and left the master and his apprentice to their spells.

"All right, Arpad, hold the boat steady and sustain me," Durril said.

The ghostly sailors manned the headland,

waiting for Arpad Zen's return as they'd promised. The damned ghost blinked into his burning form for an instant only once in all the time the wizard and his apprentice traveled up the coast. Already the marines had set a beacon at another point along the treacherous shore. They could do nothing about the burning ghost in the lighthouse.

"Ready, Arpad?" Durril asked.

"Yes, Master."

Durril cast his observation spell with practiced ease. It had become second nature with him after his time under the sea. The wizard clearly saw the agony of the innocent sailors. The last of the sunlight caused them to pulsate a vicious indigo touched with crimson. The wizard chanted, summoning the ghosts toward the boat. They floated out from the headland in a great rippling wave of ectoplasm, dipping low to skim above the water.

As they came near the small vessel, the specters formed into a wedge. At its point rode Captain Korrgan.

"You have returned, Arpad Zen," the ghostly captain said with approval. "We are grateful."

"This is my master, Durril," the apprentice replied. "He is here, as I promised."

"My apprentice's word is my bond, Captain. Are you ready?"

"We are ready, master wizard Durril. We thank you."

Zen held the boat as steady as he could while Durril chanted his most powerful exorcism spell. Each of the miserable specters presented himself before the wizard to be dissolved. At the moment of its passing, a sigh of relief floated away to mingle with the surf crashing against the hard reef. Soon there was only the sound of the water beating against the rocks. Durril slumped down in the boat.

"Master?" Arpad Zen said, concerned that Durril looked exhausted. The wizard's face was drawn.

"I am fine. Do not worry yourself." Durril dismissed Zen's solicitations with a gesture.

"Now we must tackle the ghost of the damned man."

In truth, Durril was hard-pressed to maintain the cloaking spell and perform the demanding exorcisms. Without Arpad Zen, he probably couldn't have done it. He did not want to risk exposure by employing his own master's skull or by using the crystal. Durril wanted to avoid another bout with Rusalka at all costs. Such strong magic would surely alert her to his whereabouts.

"The burning ghost's problem is far more difficult than that of the sailors, I fear," the wizard said, more to himself than to his apprentice.

Durril searched the night-shrouded headland for the ectoplasmic presence of the lighthouse beacon. It was easily located, and the wizard was disturbed at what he saw. He studied the specter for some time, probing it carefully with the observation spell.

"Just as I thought, Arpad. When the man was cursed, that old wizard placed a strong warding spell around his work to prevent any attempt at exorcism. You did well to get a transmutation spell to work against such odds," Durril said thoughtfully.

"What will you do, Master?" Zen asked, his

voice betraying his pleasure at Durril's compliment.

"You will have to sustain me, and I will have to use my own master's knowledge, even though that is dangerous. The warding can be broken, but it will take some time," the wizard replied.

"Then it cannot be done," Arpad Zen lamented.

"You cannot aid me?" Durril asked.

"No, it's not that. Of course I will do my best to help you," Zen hurried to explain. "Your master's skull is lost with your kit. I am sorry."

"It was, Arpad," Durril said as he retrieved the skull from the secret pocket in his sleeve. "I did not have all bad fortune under the sea," he concluded.

"How—"

"I will tell the whole of it later, when we are taking our ease in Wonne," Durril replied. "For now, let's get to work. Our business here is unfinished."

It took quite some time for Durril to undo the warding of the old wizard's work. When he had, the damned man burned brightly in the lighthouse, a beacon for all to see. Durril immediately began chanting the spell of exorcism, but the cursing itself had been a strong one. The ghost stubbornly refused to dissolve.

"Arpad, you must cast the spell with me," Durril ordered. "Leave the boat to its own devices and help me in this."

Surprised at his master's command, Zen did as instructed. As the wizard and his apprentice worked the exorcism together, Durril drawing on the power of his own master's knowledge, the burning ghost flickered. It alternated burning brightly and then dimly several times. At last it was released.

An exalted scream came to Durril and Zen, a faint echo on the evening breeze—and the cursed specter existed no more.

Master and apprentice sank down into the boat, their tiredness claiming them.

Morasha came alongside, leaping and playing. "What do we do now, Master Durril?" she asked.

"We wait, Morasha. We can row out to sea, but I would hesitate to get too far away from land, even this island, now," the wizard said. He did not explain about the vortex or the sea nymph's wrath.

"What we need is a ship to rescue us," he continued. "We were on our way to Wonne. It still seems like a good destination. But I don't know how to attract a vessel," he admitted.

Arpad Zen dozed in the stern of the tiny boat as night gathered around them. The day's strenuous work had been too much for the apprentice. Durril let him sleep. A group of dolphins waited nearby, jumping and diving.

"Master," Morasha said. "I have a problem and I . . . we need your help."

"We?" Durril's full attention focused on her because of the way she spoke.

The familiar briefly explained her condition to the wizard. Durril listened carefully.

"I promised her I would leave, Master Durril, when I found you. I told Saemo that you knew enough to make things right," the familiar pleaded.

"Morasha, I don't know what to do," Durril said. "I have never heard of this happening with a familiar. It can only be that the dolphin is intelligent. Most familiars inhabit bodies of less intelligent hosts. I now see why. Can Saemo tolerate your stay a while longer without harm?"

"Yes, Master Durril. I've explained to her the problem we face. I could not allow her to think I'd lied," the familiar said. She swam around and rested her snout on the side of the boat. A large eye stared at Durril.

"I will not change form if it means her death," she said. "I have promised her that. If I cannot leave her, she and I will have to remain together until her natural end." Morasha spoke with strong conviction.

"Very well. I will do the best I can to help, of course. But this is truly beyond my knowledge. We must get to Wonne, without delay. The Great Library is located there. If we are lucky, perhaps some knowledge about your condition has been recorded along with a method of relief," Durril said, trying his best to encourage the familiar—and himself. Truly, he had no idea how to proceed in this delicate matter.

"We need a ship! I will try to summon one," Durril continued. He worked carefully and well. Late in the night, the trading ship *Medici* entered the perilous waters surrounding Pellas' island.

Quickly, the wizard invoked a minor fire spell, using one oar for a torch. In no time, the *Medici* responded to his distress signal. Durril, along with Arpad Zen, was hauled aboard. Morasha and the dolphins escorted the ship.

With a brief explanation, Durril arranged their passage to Wonne, trading navigation of the ship around the reefs for two fares. Although the marines' beacon shone brightly, the waters remained extremely dangerous. All charts of the area had been lost long ago, like so much else in the Spell Wars.

Durril, with Morasha's help, led the ship away from the menacing coast and into safe waters. Captain Doge, the jovial, round little skipper of the *Medici* furnished his new guests cramped but adequate quarters and good food along with a promise to deliver them safely to the rich trading city and its many delights.

Arpad Zen fretted in the bow of the *Medici* as Morasha sported with one of the larger males of the dolphin group.

"It's unseemly," he complained to Durril, who chuckled quietly at his apprentice's sudden puritanical bent.

"I will leave you to your worries," the wizard said.

Arpad Zen did not hear his master. He was too busy scowling at Morasha.

Durril made his way to the stern of the ship where he could rest alone and take stock of his situation.

Captain Doge had insisted on paying him for his navigational services, saying that rescue at sea was a duty. Durril jingled the small purse containing a half dozen gold coins. His party would not arrive penniless in Wonne. Durril took a deep breath, drinking in the cool, tangy night air. He rejoiced in the ease of it. For too long he had been threatened with suffocation.

Morasha and Arpad Zen were reunited with him. Morasha's circumstances presented a problem, one of the more intriguing ones Durril had encountered as a wizard. With the problem came opportunity. He looked forward to finding the answer to her dilemma in Wonne's Great Library.

It had been many years since the wizard had researched there as a student. For a moment Durril was caught in the embrace of memory. Thoughts of youth and his anticipation of adventure flooded over him. His life had worked out well so far. He had to admit that it was certainly rich in adventure.

Durril lounged in the fantail, pleased with the world. Once the ship cleared Pellas' island, he dropped the cloaking spell. He rested easily now, his memories taking him away from the strain of the magic and his recent ordeal.

Arpad Zen was proving to be much more adroit than the wizard had originally believed. Perhaps a potential lurked there that both master and apprentice had overlooked. Somehow, Zen's treacherously inept storytelling would have to be checked, though.

Most of all, Durril had grown in his own ability. Under the sea, his skills had sharpened. When he worked now, the spells cut like the honed edge of a deftly wielded sword. Miraculously, he had regained his own master's skull. And there was the enigmatic crystal.

The wizard paused in his musings, retrieving the crystal from its hiding place.

He held it in his left hand. He attempted once more to see its substance. Nothing. Then it started warming his hand.

"At last," a voice whispered, causing Durril to start and look about the deck. He saw no one. He stood alone on the fantail under the stars.

"At last, you have come to release me."

The voice came from the crystal, which grew warmer in Durril's grasp.

"What are you?" the wizard asked.

"I am the substance of the grand wizard, Rahn'dom."

"Rahn'dom? But you disappeared long ago. Some say you are nothing more than a legend," Durril said, perplexed.

"When I forged the ancient sword of iron, I transferred my substance to the black stone in its pommel. There I defeated those who would use the sword's power for evil purposes. I also escaped those who wished my death. Alas, I failed to save my wife and daughter from their corruption," the voice lamented; then it strengthened. "Evil desired this world long ago and I fought its grasp."

"But—" Durril began.

"Do not interrupt. There is little time," said Rahn'dom. "Only one who would use the sword against the evil which threatens this world could wield it. Him I would aid in return for my release. Having no other get of my loins, he would also be my heir."

"I ask your name," Rahn'dom said.

"Durril, master wizard of the Plenn Archipelagoes," Durril managed to respond.

"You shall inherit my powers, Durril. They will not all come to you at once, but only as you grow in understanding. I am cautious even now."

"Why me?" Durril asked, frightened of Rahn'dom's answer.

"The one who retrieved the sword from the protection of the Mother Ocean is the one who would release me. That one might also grow into my inheritance. I can now depart from my crystal prison, knowing my knowledge will live for good. I made sure of these protections, believe me, Durril. The time for my dissolution was right when this stone touched air once again. I will take my leave from you now. Bear the mark of my favor."

Before Durril could speak, before he could question the stone and the wizard within, it burst apart into a fine, shining powder, and dissolved in his hand. A gust of wind took it, scattering the glistening powder far out over the sea.

As the wizard's hand cooled, it shone with the silver traces of the crystal's passage, a permanent mark embedded forever in Durril's skin.

Durril made a fist, hiding the mark of power as he stared into the dark water. He tried to make sense of the crystal and its unexpected transformation. Now he had a double reason for his search in the Great Library.

"Rahn'dom?" he said quietly to the billowing waves. Durril noticed a phosphorescence surrounding the *Medici*. It followed the ship. Durril's hand itched, his palm warm. The silver marking burned brighter. The meaning of this new warning came to him with a flash of insight.

"Rusalka!" Durril exclaimed.

The wizard leaned over the rail, straining to locate the sea nymph. His purse of gold coins jingled at his waist.

The sea nymph rose out of the water, her chariot drawn by two sea horses whose flaming trail marked the dark water behind the merchanter. Her burnished hair wrapped about her pale body like delicate strands of seaweed.

"Durril, are you really leaving me?" Rusalka enticed with a voice made of ancient lures.

"Yes, Rusalka, forever," Durril replied.

He opened the captain's purse and counted out half its contents. As was customary in days of yore, he tossed the coins to her.

"For safe passage," the wizard said.

The sea nymph deftly caught the shining gold.

"For safe passage this time, my love," she agreed.

Smiling at Durril, she sank slowly beneath the waves as her phosphorescent escort circled away from the ship.

Rusalka, Durril knew, would challenge him again should he pass this way. For now, she had accepted his payment. He had escaped the circle of her power and regained the surface. Did she fear his powers above the Mother Ocean's waves? Possibly. He was left wondering what she intended. Rusalka, for all her professed love, still nurtured the tiny spark of greed and ambition that had once ruined the world.

She wanted her wizard back—and would never stop trying to lure Durril back to her undersea kingdom.

"Durril," Arpad Zen interrupted, the apprentice's unhappiness plainly showing. "Look at that. It is unseemly, I tell you. Make her stop. I would wring her neck if I had the chance," Zen said angrily.

Dancing past the ship, Morasha frolicked with her male companion.

Durril wondered at this strange turn, but he took pity on his apprentice.

"Arpad, I've been meaning to ask how you did that transmutation spell. It was a good idea."

Torn between his master's compliment and his frustration with Morasha, Zen launched into a detailed description of his spell casting. Durril immediately regretted his decision to distract the apprentice from Morasha's antics.

"Tukker was going to kill me, Master, and I had never exorcised anything except the poltergeists, but I had to do something because I knew that the wreckers had little use for me so I tried everything I knew how, but I hadn't listened to you well enough and I couldn't remember the spells I've watched you do. I have promised myself to be a better student, Master Durril, and I promise the same to you now—"

"Arpad!" Durril snapped in spite of himself.

"Oh yes, the transmutation spell," the apprentice said, remembering that his master had asked a question.

"Tukker locked me in the lighthouse the night after he had me bound and gagged because he didn't want to hear the joke about the traveling salesman and the peg-legged whore from Pin and so I had to do something with the burning ghost but I couldn't think of anything.

"I guess you can say it all began when I kicked the bucket . . ."

The End?

The end of a book is never really *the end* for a person who reads. He or she can always open another. And another.

Every page holds possibilities.

But millions of kids don't see them. Don't know they're there. Millions of kids can't read, or won't.

That's why there's RIF. Reading is Fundamental (RIF) is a national nonprofit program that works with thousands of community organizations to help young people discover the fun—and the importance—of reading.

RIF motivates kids so that they *want* to read. And RIF works directly with parents to help them encourage their children's reading. RIF gets books to children and children into books, so they grow up reading and become adults who can read. Adults like you.

For more information on how to start a RIF program in your neighborhood, or help your own child grow up reading, write to:

RIF
Dept. BK-1
Box 23444
Washington, D.C.
20026

Founded in 1966, RIF is a national non-profit organization with local projects run by volunteers in every state of the union.

OUTPASSAGE
JANET MORRIS & CHRIS MORRIS

It could have been the ultimate in blind dates,
but before Dennis Cox and Paige Barnett can
cement their mutual attraction for each other,
they are shanghaied to a backwater planet
where a fermenting rebellion threatens IST's
mining interests as well as the planet's existence. Drawn together in their mutual desire
for truth and justice, Dennis and Paige battle
he unknown in an epic adventure complete with
New Age space war, politics, and spirituality.

ISBN: 0-517-00832-7 $3.50

AN INTERSTELLAR EXPERIENCE

ON SALE NOW!

NEENA GATHERING

VALERIE NIEMAN COLANDER

It's the twenty-first century and America is no more. The U.S. has split into sections and destroyed itself with chemical warfare. A civilization based on technology, communications, mass transportation, factories, schools, culture, and medicine has ceased to exist. Forced to grow up quickly under such conditions, can Neena eke out a living while fighting off roving bands of survivors as well as the misguided attention of her uncle, Ted? Or will she choose to become the symbol of a reborn nation with the horribly scarred but loving Arden?

ISBN: 0-517-00643-X   Price: $2.95